Home Wrecker

Home Wrecker

Dwayne S. Joseph

www.urbanbooks.net

Urban Books, LLC
78 East Industry Court
Deer Park, NY 11729

ISBN-13: 978-1-60162-317-1
ISBN-10: 1-60162-317-8

First Mass Market Printing September 2011
First Trade Paperback Printing September 2008
Printed in the United States of America

10 9 8 7 6 5 4 3 2 1

Distributed by Kensington Publishing Corp.
Submit Wholesale Orders to:
Kensington Publishing Corp.
C/O Penguin Group (USA) Inc.
Attention: Order Processing
405 Murray Hill Parkway
East Rutherford, NJ 07073-2316
Phone: 1-800-526-0275
Fax: 1-800-227-9604

Acknowledgments

I'm a writer.

I've been writing since I was thirteen years old. I started out with horror fiction. I moved to mystery/thriller fiction next. As the years passed, I ended up doing relationship drama fiction, or contemporary fiction as it's also called. The types of stories I've told have changed, but one thing has remained the same: my goal to improve and get better with each one that I do. Each book begins a new competition that I have with myself. Can I get better? Can I create better characters? Can the drama become more intense? More importantly, can my writing improve? With each book I set out to answer those questions with a resounding "Yes!" If you've been keeping up with me on my literary journey, hopefully you've been able to see growth. That's important to me. People often ask for advice for new or aspiring authors. One piece of advice I have is to respect the craft of writing. By respecting it, you will want to improve on it. You will want to be better.

That brings me to *Home Wrecker*.

For those who've read my earlier works (I thank you from the bottom of my heart, by the way!), you are going to notice three things. One: it's not the usual relationship drama. Two: it's a much more adult novel, much more intense. Three: hopefully you will feel as though I've really grown as an author. *Home Wrecker* is a complete turn away from anything I've done in the past, and that's because I couldn't allow myself to be tied down to doing one type of story. Relationship drama was/is fun, but I have much more in my repertoire.

I've never created a character as fierce, sexy, arrogant, or even as cold as Lisette. She walks it like she talks it, and she has no time for anyone that likes to play around. She'll literally chew you up, spit you out into the middle of a busy intersection and keep on walking as though you never existed. I had a lot of fun with her and all of the other characters in the story. They are a memorable bunch that will surprise you (At least if I did my job right they will). I hope you enjoy their company as much as I did, because we've had a lot of laughs together during this process.

I have to thank God first and foremost for bringing Lisette to me. My writing goes where He takes it. I am grateful.

Wendy and my rug rats Tati, Nati, and Xavier: your support, friendship, and love mean everything. I appreciate you and love you!! My family: Love you guys! Nicole . . . even though you're a Cowboys fan . . . you too! Thanks to all of you for being there. Granny and Grandmother . . . the matriarchs: I love you both!! Aleah . . . thanks so much for reading the books. I had no idea!!

To my friends: The best! 'Nuff said. To the Friday night Xbox 360 crew: Chris, G-Money, Shawny poop, Jay, Rusty, Billy Bob, Josh, Scott (Mr. Incognegro), and Steve . . . I have one thing to say: "Bring your A game, because I have headshots coming!" Eric, welcome to the 360 side of the force! Daren, we're waiting for you! La Jill Hunt . . . continue to do your thing. Write!!! Perón Long . . . congrats, man. Now the fun really starts. Portia Cannon . . . It's really time to go to work now!

To the book clubs: Sweet Soul Sisters, One Book @ A Time, The African Violets Book Club, C.A.T.T.S., African American Sisters In Spirit, Sisters In Spirit II, Brown Sugar Sistahs With Books, Page Turnas Book Club, For Da Sista's Book Club,

Aminia Book Club, Circle of Women, Ujima Nia, Sister 2 Sister, Ebony Jewels Book Club, Sistahs On The Reading Edge, Cushcity.com, Between The Covers Literary Group, B~More Readers With W.I.S.D.O.M., The Woman In Me 2002 Book Club, Cyrus A Webb and the Conversations Book Club, Nubian Sistas Book Club. It has truly been an honor for me to have met with you all. I cannot thank you enough for the great time and honest feedback that you all provided. If you thought we had things to discuss before . . . wait until you finish this one!

I cannot thank you all enough for your hospitality, your spirited conversations, your friendship, and most of all, your support. Meeting with all of you is always a good time! I'm blessed and honored that you have chosen my books to read, review and discuss! I can't wait!!

To Nancy Silvas, Jocelyn Lawson, Lisa McManuels, Omedia Cutler, Dana Bowles, Portia Cannon . . . thank you all for the feedback and letting me know that I was on to something! I appreciated the patience as you waited to see what was going to happen next!!

To the readers and people who've hit me up on MySpace, thank you for every bit of feedback that you give. Receiving those e-mails and messages mean the world to me. Please keep them coming. And don't forget to post those reviews for all of us in the literary game. Michelle Princeluva79 . . . thank you! Poetic Author Casche Russell . . . keep doing it! Sonya Sparks . . . enjoy the ride!

To my New York Giants: I'm getting my G-Men tattoo soon because I'm a lifer!! Go Big Blue! Ok. Enough. Now get to reading. Peace!

Dwayne S. Joseph

DJoseph21044@gmail.com
www.myspace.com/DwayneSJoseph

Lisette

1

I'm a home wrecker I tear families apart with seduction. A subtle smile somewhere between innocence and raw sex. Home wrecker. C-cup breasts. Twenty-five inch waist. An ass that Beyoncé would envy. That's what I use to lure men away. Call me the pied piper. Or better yet, the pied pipestress. Home wrecker. I'm good at what I do. I'm not a whore. I'm not a woman desperate for affection. I'm not a friend with benefits. I'm not a mistress. Breaking up marriages is my profession. Wives pay me to set up their husbands. Pay good money.

Thousands for a few hours of my time. That's about how long it takes me to get a man to forget about the ring on his finger and say to hell with the vows he made. A few hours and then he's lost it all. In most cases, it's his money, his home, his car, his family. In other cases, it's his manhood.

And I don't mean that he becomes John Wayne Bobbitt's distant cousin.

Most women have their men set up because they're tired of being disrespected. They spend their days and nights catering to their men. Cooking, cleaning, taking care of the kids, sexing when it's required. They do all of this, yet they're constantly having to deal with lies, deceit, physical and emotional abuse. They suffer day after day, wondering why a man they gave their all to would hurt them the way they do. They suffer until they can't take it anymore.

Then they call me.

They want the son-of-a-bitch trapped. Caught on tape. They want pictures. Sometimes they want to be in the room, watching, getting a firsthand view of their men doing what most of them knew they'd do. Of course, some still hold out hope that their men will change their minds at the last minute because they love their wives just too much to betray them. But that never happens, because I don't allow it to happen. In the end, the bastard's caught and papers are served.

Game over.

That's when a man loses it all.

They lose their manhood, however, when their women have them set up strictly for power and control. These women never have any intention of divorcing their men. See, instead of presenting the evidence and taking half, they hold that evidence over their men's heads. Whatever they want, they get. Whenever they want it, it's theirs. No complaints about how much the piece of jewelry or a new pair of shoes cost. No put downs. No mouth at all, because while their men are doing or spending whatever it takes to keep from having to give up their houses or cars, or to avoid shelling out thousands in child support (millions in some cases), the women get free reign to go and fuck the pool boy, the gardener, or the sexy gym instructor with the tight ass.

Flip the coin and the side's the same. Either way you look at it, my services provide financial stability. Most of all, I give back what most of my clients should have never lost: control.

Some prefer the other option, but for a lot of women—at least the ones that deal with me—replacing that is better than getting half any day.

Past

2

Setting up men for a living was never in my career plan, but when I look back on my past, it's obvious that I was always headed down that road. See, at thirteen years old, I understood I had power over men.

Equipped with a seventeen-year-old's curvaceous and fully developed body, I realized back then that all it took to get what I wanted was a subtle, seductive smile, a sexy gaze, or a you-know-you-want-it stance.

My father was the first man I learned to control.

Most people assumed I had him wrapped around my finger because he loved me unconditionally. I was his daughter, his princess, but I knew better. My father was a pervert, who was always taking side glances at me and looking me up and down. He used to love to accidentally walk in on me when I was showering or getting undressed. But instead of excusing himself and leaving right away, he would take long, lingering seconds to admire "how grown" his little girl was. He never touched me improperly, but I could see in his eyes that he wanted to fuck me good.

I should have been uncomfortable and disgusted by the fact that my own father had sexual thoughts about me, but I never was. I was amused, actually. I mean, there I was, a thirteen-year-old girl getting a rise out of a grown man—hell, my own father!

Toying with him, I learned the art of seduction and garnered a true understanding of the type of power I possessed then. With an inviting look, a seductive smile, a sexy stance, I realized I could get whatever I wanted.

Through my father, I understood just how weak men were. I learned that if you teased them just enough, their imaginations would run wild, their dicks would swell, and they'd become puppets doing whatever it was you wanted them to.

My mother saw the power I had over my father and tried time and time again to stand in my way. But although I was young, I'd been too in-tune with my sex appeal. By the time I was fifteen, she left my father and me. She never admitted it, but I think she was jealous of the fact that, up until his fatal heart attack, I could have still manipulated the hell out him.

Manipulation.

Break it down.

A woman must have come up with the word.

I continued to learn and love the power of manipulation through my teenage years and on into my early twenties. There was just nothing as intense to me as pulling a man's strings to get what I wanted without having to give up anything in return. And that was always the case. Boys and men bought me things, took me places, and did anything I told them to, and unless I wanted it to happen, they never even got a whiff of my pussy.

Manipulation.

Control.

The words are synonymous.

Playing men was always like a game to me, because I never really needed them.

I came to the realization in my early teens that in order for me to truly have control over a man, I had to be independent and successful. A woman that could play a man, but didn't have her own shit got no respect from me, because in my eyes they were weak-minded. They may have had the tits and ass and knew how to use them, but they lacked intelligence, because if they were truly us-ing their brains, they would realize that a woman who had her own shit was far more desirable.

See, men are simple. They do all of their rationalization with their dicks, and think that because God gave them chest hair, they're supposed be the dominant ones.

A woman that needs nothing is a woman most wanted because she's viewed as a challenge. Bring your own car into the relationship—a man will want to buy you a better, more expensive one. Have your own home—a man will want you to move into his. Have your own money and he'll say to hell with the price and empty out his own wallet.

Men are driven by the need to impress. Women who understand this are the ones that get the most respect from me.

My mother, as beautiful as she was, never brought anything to the table, which is why my father never truly respected her. She always used to complain about how I was just like my father. I guess she's been right, because I didn't have much respect for her either. To this day, we still don't have much of a relationship.

Like I said, I never intended on becoming a home wrecker.

Prior to my career change, I was the head buyer for LeVor Fashions—an up and coming urban fashion company that was bringing some serious heat to the powerhouses like Sean John and Rocawear. On a day-to-day basis, I met with established designers as well as new, fresh ones and basically said yay or nay to the ideas they'd come up with. LeVor was doing great before I got there, but I can't lie—I had a lot to do with the company's growth over a four year period.

I always had a keen eye when it came to fashion. I just knew what did and didn't look good. What would or wouldn't work. To me, style went hand in hand with the power a woman possessed. It was all part of the package.

During my junior year in college, I was able to land an internship with LeVor, starting out as an assistant for the head buyer at that time. While I did the minute tasks like making copies, putting away files, and running errands, my mentor would allow me to get into the thick of things by seeking out my opinion, which actually mattered. Under her, I learned the do's and don'ts of the industry, and I got a true understanding of trends and how to recognize what they were and when they would happen.

During my senior year, I was given my first major task of choosing the design for a pair of jeans the company was going to kick off their summer line with. The pair I chose was supposed to be the teaser, but it turned out to be their biggest seller for the season. Impressed with everything I'd done during my internship, LeVor hired me as a junior level buyer after I graduated.

I did that for three years and enjoyed great success in my role, until I was suddenly propelled to head buyer when my mentor quit unexpectedly and went to work for the competition. So there I was at twenty-six, the youngest person in the company, with an executive position. I had a six-figure salary, drove a Mercedes, and owned a luxurious condo overlooking the city. I was a single and successful bad-ass, honey complected black woman, and the men loved and hated me. They loved me because I had the beauty and the brains. They hated me because I couldn't be tamed.

Remember: control was what it was all about for me.

Life was good for me back then. Shit, life was great. Especially my career. I was respected.

I was envied. I never expected my career to change.

But then I went to Texas.

3

Houston, Texas. Sofitel Hotel. At the bar in the lounge, sitting with the VP of marketing, Marlene Stewart.

That was where my career changed.

We were having drinks. Me, a Cosmopolitan. Marlene, white wine. We were in Houston attending the fashion show of one of the country's hottest female rappers—XXXstacy. Like P. Diddy, Jay Z, and other rappers with huge followings, XXXstacy decided to expand her tiny empire and step into the world of fashion. She didn't design shit, but with her name, XXXstacy Wear was destined to blow up.

Some top people at LeVor received insider information about XXXstacy's desire to get into fashion and with relentless pursuit, the company managed to work out a deal with XXXstacy that would be beneficial to both sides.

Houston was XXXstacy's hometown, so it was naturally the site for the premier showing. I'd designed some and approved much of what the public was going to see. Marlene had been responsible for the buzz. Countless hours put in, XXXstacy Wear was more our baby than XXX-stacy's herself. After one too many last minute meetings, we were in the lounge winding down before the big showing the next day.

Marlene was an attractive, older, white female in her mid-forties that could have easily passed for mid-thirties. She was an obsessive woman. Obsessive about her work. Obsessive about her body. Obsessive about her husband.

"Fucking asshole." Marlene snapped her cell phone shut.

I looked at her, but didn't say anything. That was the fifth time in the past seven minutes that she'd done that. I took a sip of my Cosmo and waited for her to curse again.

"Fucking asshole. He's probably fucking her right now." Marlene angrily passed her hand through her shoulder-length brown hair.

I took another sip of my drink, blotted the corner of my mouth with my thumb and index finger, and said, "Why don't you just divorce him?"

Marlene frowned. "And deal with the scrutiny from friends and family? No thank you."

"But he's fucking his secretary."

As I said that, a man sitting on the stool beside Marlene looked in our direction. I told him to mind his business with my eyes. He got up and left.

Marlene sipped her wine and gave an irritated smile. "Yes, he is. Unfortunately I've never been able to prove that."

"No e-mails? No text messages?"

"No secret love notes. Nothing."

"So how do you know for certain that he's fucking her?"

Marlene gave me a come-on-now look. "You know as a woman we just know. Besides, I can smell her pussy on him whenever he's been with her. It's kind of tart, like maybe she only cleans it once a day."

I wrinkled my nose. "That's nasty."

"She's nasty. The skinny bitch. Smiling in my face whenever I see her, as if she's really pulling something over on me. Pathetic."

"Maybe she's smiling because she knows you know," I said, raising my eyebrows.

"Then she's a skinny, pathetic, arrogant bitch for thinking her inexperienced pussy is that good."

I took a sip again and nodded. "Inexperienced or not, Marlene, it must be something to have your husband swimming in it."

Marlene looked at me. My honesty had stung. She flipped open her cell again.

"Why are you calling him?"

Marlene hit the TALK button to send the call. "I don't know," she said, her voice filled with frustration.

I frowned. Shook my head. I never understood why women did that. Stressed over a man.

"Fucking asshole." Marlene slammed her phone down on the bar counter.

"Why did you marry him, Marlene?"

"You've seen him. Thirty, a face as pretty as Brad Pitt, a body as delicious as the Rock's."

"So he's attractive. That can't be the only reason you married him."

Marlene looked at me, then down at her phone and sighed. "He can fuck."

"What?"

"I said, he can fuck."

I spit out a little of the Cosmo and laughed. "Are you serious? That's why you married him?"

Marlene passed her hand through her hair again, something she did when she was aggravated. "I've been married twice before, Lisette, to men who were my age and were on my level, both mentally and financially. They were nice, decent men. Good conversationalists. Driven. Had good credit. Pretty much what you'd want in a man."

I shrugged my shoulders. "So what was the problem?"

"For all of the good qualities they had, there was one problem. A major problem."

"Let me guess . . . they couldn't fuck."

"They had dicks, but had no clue how to use them."

I couldn't help but laugh.

"I'm serious, Lisette! They were so unfamiliar with their own tool, that I spent too many damn nights taking care of myself after they were supposed to. It was frustrating. Eventually I got tired of fucking myself and started fucking other men. My first husband caught me cheating. That's why the marriage ended. I divorced my second husband before he could catch me."

I laughed again, finished off my Cosmo, and cued the bartender with my index finger for another. "So Steve put it on you, huh?"

"Steve fucks like he invented it. I met him at the gym. He used to pursue me daily. At first I used to brush him off. I mean, I'm almost fifty. I couldn't possibly mess with a man fifteen years my junior, right?"

"But you did."

"He was persistent. Always approaching me with his sexy ways and his sexy pretty boy smile. Always ready with the compliments. I finally gave in one day, and agreed to go out with him to dinner. I figured, what was the harm? It was just dinner."

"I'm guessing it turned into a long dinner and an early breakfast."

Marlene closed her eyes briefly. I could tell that she was reminiscing. "Lisette," she said, opening her eyes, "I didn't plan on sleeping with him that night, but with the alcohol, his looks, and the fact that it had been months since I'd had any, we ended up going back to my place."

"And you were ready to marry him the next day, right?"

Marlene finished her wine, did the same finger motion to the bartender, and said, "Trust me. . . . If you fucked Steve, you'd be hooked too."

I closed my eyes a bit. "I doubt that."

"Steve's good, honey. Damn good."

"And now the secretary is getting some."

"Yes. The bitch."

"And instead of having to hear any crap about being divorced for a third time, you're calling him practically every five minutes?"

Closing her cell again, Marlene said, "Yes. I don't need to hear the shit from anyone. I don't want to deal with the judgmental stares. Of all of my friends and family, I'm the one who can't keep a man."

"Have you tried catching him in the act?"

"Of course. Surprise visits to his office. I've come home a day or days early from business trips."

"And you've never caught him?"

"Never."

"But he comes home smelling like tart pussy?"

"Yes."

The bartender brought our drinks and flashed us a smile. He was an attractive brother with an athletic build. Watching his muscles flex, I wondered if he could fuck the way Marlene said Steve could. I stopped wondering when he walked over to a man sitting three bar stools down from us and gave him just too much attention.

Always the good looking ones.

I looked back at Marlene. She was a mess. Attractive. Fit. Successful. Yet she was irritated and jealous because a man she knew she was too good for was giving her dick away.

I took a swallow of my fresh Cosmo. "Why don't you just set him up?"

"Excuse me?"

"Set him up. Hire a hooker to fuck him."

"I can't do that."

"Why?"

"Because it's wrong."

"You could have been in an accident and that's why you're calling him constantly. Isn't it wrong that he's ignoring your calls?"

Marlene didn't answer.

I continued. "Isn't it wrong that you're emotionally stressed from the fact that the man you married is giving your dick away? The dick that he vowed would only be yours?"

Marlene looked at her phone, whispered, "Fucking asshole."

"Forget a hooker," I said. "A hooker's not good enough.

He can pass that off as a mistake. A one time lapse in judgment. He's human. It wouldn't happen again. What you need is a friend. A friend is much worse. She can say he'd been coming on to her behind your back. She can say that he'd promised to give her what he gives to you."

"Lisette . . . are you serious?"

"Your friend can say that he'd threatened to flip the script by telling you that she was the one coming on to him. You wouldn't take her word over his because he loves you. That's what your friend can say came from his mouth."

"Lisette . . ."

"Do you have a friend that would do that?"

"Lisette . . . I . . . I can't."

"Why not?"

"Because."

"Catch him in the act with someone you know, and your friends and family can't say shit."

"But . . . but . . ."

Marlene paused and fiddled with her glass.

"But what, Marlene? Do you want to continue being unhappy?"

"No."

"Do you want to continue playing second fiddle to tart-smelling pussy?"

"No," Marlene said.

"Then set him up. Get someone that you trust."

"But . . . but . . ."

"But what, Marlene?"

"But . . . I don't have any friends that I trust like that."

Silence overtook our conversation as Marlene watched me watching her.

Set him up.

Set him up and no one could say shit.

That's all she had to do to regain control.

I stared at her intensely. Marlene was a good woman. Honest and down-to-earth. Like any other woman, all she wanted was to be loved, respected, and to get some good dick. She didn't deserve Steve's shit.

"I'll do it," I said.

Marlene's eyes widened. "What?"

"I'll do it. I'll set him up."

"You?"

"Yes. He knows me. I've been to your house a few times. He's had opportunities to come on to me."

"But, Lisette . . ."

"Do you or do you not want out of this marriage?"

Marlene opened her mouth to protest, but instead dropped her chin to her chest. "Yes," she said.

And there it was.

She wanted out.

I could make it happen.

That's when my career changed.

4

"I'll pay you."

I looked at Marlene. "Excuse me?"

"I . . . I'll pay you for . . . you know . . . helping me."

We were still in the lounge. At a table this time. Sitting in a corner, away from bartenders and strangers trying to eavesdrop without making it obvious, but doing a terrible job. A small candle flickered in the middle of the table between us. Soft music sighed from speakers.

The lounge had dim lighting. That, combined with the candle's flame, cast an eerie shadow across Marlene's pale face. She was looking off to the right, too embarrassed or ashamed, or both, to look at me.

"Are you calling me a whore, Marlene?"

Marlene's head snapped back in my direction. "What?"

"You're offering to pay me to trap your husband. Am I a prostitute in your eyes?"

Marlene's mouth popped open. "Oh God, no! No! I didn't mean . . . Oh God, no! Please, I . . . I didn't mean to imply . . .

I just . . . just figured . . ." Marlene paused, passed her hand through her hair, took a healthy sip of her wine, looked down at the designs in the tablecloth, and then back at me. "I'm . . . I'm sorry, Lisette. I didn't mean to be disrespectful. Please forget I said that. Just forget I said anything at all."

I watched her, but didn't respond. She reeked of unhappiness. Her shoulders were slumped, her head was bowed, her body shuddered as she began to cry. She was defeated. Her posture. Her demeanor.

This was why I stayed away from relationships. Relationships made you dependent. Being dependent meant you had no control.

One time.

I tried it one time.

I was eighteen. He was twenty-one.

He was Denzel handsome. Had P. Diddy's style. Possessed 50 Cent's body and attitude before Fiddy ever stepped on the scene. He appealed to me on a level no one else had before.

I wasn't myself when I was with him. All of the power I had was gone. I fell for him hard. Fell for his attitude, his style and his looks. He was sure of himself in a way that no guy I'd dealt with before had been.

Had I been born a man, I would have been him.

We dated for two years. The first six months were bliss. He was sweet, loving and considerate. Then month seven came and the tsunami hit. Sweet, loving, and considerate disappeared. Ignorant, controlling, and abusive took its place.

Eighteen months.

That's how long it took before I woke up from whatever spell I'd fallen under and got medieval on his ass. He hit me, and I'd finally hit back. He kicked. I kicked. He tried to strangle me, I sent his balls up into his throat, Mike Tyson'd his hand. Things got ugly.

Very ugly.

To this day, I'm not sure why I put up with the emotional and physical abuse, but I am sure of one thing: if another motherfucker ever puts his hands on me, they better pray they kill me.

Relationships.

Looking at Marlene was all the justification I needed for avoiding them.

"How much, Marlene? How much would you pay to get out of your marriage?"

Marlene looked at me. Her mascara had run from her crying. She shook her head. "Lisette . . . I . . . I didn't mean—"

"How much, Marlene?" I said, cutting her off.

"I . . . I don't know."

"Ten thousand. Are you willing to pay that much? What about fifteen? How unhappy are you? How much do you want out of this?"

Marlene grabbed a napkin, blotted her eyes, and frowned at the mascara stain left behind.

"Twenty thousand," I continued. "To get him out of your life. Twenty-five thousand to make sure you're family can't scrutinize. Thirty thousand so that he doesn't get shit from you. How badly do you want out?"

Marlene stared at me. I stared at Marlene. This should have been an odd conversation for me. I was offering to trap a man for money. The conversation should have been awkward.

But it wasn't.

For some reason, it felt like everything I had ever gone through in my life, everything I'd ever done or said, had all led up to this moment in Houston, Texas, at the Sofitel Hotel.

"I . . . I would need evidence," Marlene said. "Something I could use against him in court."

I closed my eyes a bit. The tone in her voice had changed. The flaccid look in her eyes was disappearing.

"What would you want me to get?"

Marlene's shoulders rose as her back straightened. "I don't want you to get anything."

"But you said you need evidence."

"I want to walk in on you fucking him."

Whoa.

Right before my eyes, Marlene had changed. The victim was gone.

"You want me to fuck him?"

"Yes. And I want to walk in on it. I'll have someone with me. A witness. They won't know what's going on. I want to walk into my home and catch you with him. I want to see you riding him. Fucking asshole. I want him out of my life."

"You've thought about this before?"

"Never. But I've dreamt it. I've watched him fuck other women over and over in my dreams."

"How badly, Marlene? Trapping is one thing. Fucking him is another."

"Fifty thousand."

My heart stopped beating momentarily.

Fifty thousand dollars.

That was a lot of money.

"Are you serious?"

"I hate him, Lisette. He disrespects me every day when he looks at me with her pussy on his breath. I want him out of my life."

"And you're willing to pay?"

"Fifty thousand dollars, yes. Are you willing to do it?"

Pink Martini was playing in the background. Their song, "Amado Mio," from their CD *Sympatique*. I had the CD at home. I loved that song. Listening to it always put me in a mood. I listened to the song as Marlene waited for her answer.

Was I willing to do it?

Fifty thousand dollars.

I closed my eyes for a sec, let the song sooth and entice me the way it did at home.

Was I willing to do it?

She said Steve fucked like he invented it. I listened to the song and wondered if it was true. Wondered if he could fuck me as good as the song soothed.

Was I willing to do it?

Fifty thousand dollars to be fucked by Pink Martini, live and in stereo.

"Yes. I'm willing."

5

"Have you done something like this before?"

"You're calling me a whore again."

Hand through her hair, Marlene said, "Sorry. I didn't mean it. I'm just nervous. Well, not nervous. Shocked. That's a better word. Aren't you shocked?"

I sipped my Cosmo. "Not really."

"How could you not be? I never would have thought I'd be having a discussion like this."

"Desperate times call for desperate measures," I said.

"Is that what I am? Desperate."

"Are you?"

Marlene ran her slender index finger around the rim of her glass. "Yes," she said, "I am."

"Why do you care so much about what your friends and family think?"

Marlene frowned. "My family can be brutal. To each member, especially the women, life is more about status and appearance than it is about happiness. I'm the black sheep of the family. I've always believed in being happy. My mother hasn't loved my father for years, but she would never leave him, even though she cheats on him as though it were her second profession. Each one of her friends are wealthy and have been married to their affluent husbands forever. God forbid my mother step outside of that circle and be with a man that treats her with respect. My sister is the same way. So are my aunts.

"When I was caught cheating on my first husband, I caught so much hell. He was educated, came from a rich, strong background. In everyone's eyes, I'd pretty much struck gold. When my secret was exposed, you would have thought the gates to hell had opened up."

"How could you be so selfish and stupid, Marlene? The man comes from good stock. Do you know what you look like running around on a man like that? Do you know how much shame you've brought to this family? People are talking. You're making us the laughing stock of this community."

"I had to hear shit like that every day. It was frustrating. It was hard. It was hurtful."

"But despite the scrutiny, you left your second husband?"

"I had this whole I-don't-give-a-fuck attitude going at that time. After having gone through it with my first husband, I figured what the hell. It'd be easier to take the lectures than to not get sexed properly, which would have ultimately led to me cheating again. So why not say 'fuck it' and leave him? It wasn't always easy, though. Some days I wished I would have just stayed with him and been more careful about fooling around."

"Did your family have anything negative to say about Steve's age?"

"No, because he was well off. Besides, I think his looks blinded everyone."

"But now you can see."

"Clearly."

Music slipped in between the conversation. Jazz. Guitar. Sounded like Norman Brown. Maybe Johnathan Butler. Wasn't sure which, but I liked it.

"So when do you want this done?" I asked.

Marlene looked at me, then off to the right, then left, then back at me. "When can you do it?"

I thought about that for a moment. As I did, a couple walked into the lounge with a baby in a car seat. I looked at them and wondered. "How come you never had children?"

Marlene shrugged. "When I was younger, I was too into my career. By the time I was ready, I had two failed marriages. When Steve and I married, I thought we were going to have at least one child, especially with the way my clock was ticking. I used to imagine having the prettiest or the most handsome baby with Steve." Hand through her hair again, she said, "Fucking asshole."

I looked over at the couple again. The mother was holding the baby in her arms—a girl draped in pink—and giving her a bottle. The father was looking over his wife's shoulder, staring at a blond female with big tits, who was sitting with an older gentleman who could have easily been her grandfather. By the way she was rubbing his leg, it was obvious that he wasn't. She reminded me of a younger Anna Nicole Smith, but not as pretty. Anna Nicole; now that was a woman who understood her power.

I looked back to the husband. I could practically see his dick in his hand. Stroking. Fantasizing. Doing things in his mind to her that he'd never do to his wife.

I thought about my father and my one-time relationship.

Men.

They were all the same.

I looked back at Marlene. "Are you on the pill?"

"The pill? No. They make me sick to my stomach. I use a diaphragm. Why?"

"Do you still want to have a baby?"

"It would have been nice being a mother, but I'm too old now."

"A woman in her sixties gave birth to twins last year. You're a spring chicken compared to her. Besides, having kids at an older age is the in thing right now."

Marlene raised her eyebrows. "Maybe so, but I wouldn't do it to be part of that crowd."

"So would you do it?"

Marlene sipped her wine, blotted her lips. "If I had the right man . . . maybe I'd give it a try."

I looked back to the husband with the roving eyes. He was still stroking, still mentally fucking Anna Nicole's copycat. I wondered if his wife noticed. Was she just so in love with her child that she was completely oblivious to her husband's attention span, or lack thereof? Or did she know and just not care, as most women didn't? I watched him. He was practically mesmerized by the double D's.

Ass. For all of the shit and disrespect a woman endured, men never suffered enough.

Steve.

He needed to suffer.

I looked back to Marlene and thought that for the power and control I was going to help her get, I should be paid.

"When you get home on Sunday night, have sex with Steve."

Marlene eyed me curiously. "Have sex?"

"Yes. And forget the diaphragm."

There was a lot of confusion in her eyes at that statement. Before she could ask, I said, "In four weeks, give me the news that you're pregnant. Make sure you've broken the news to Steve first. Two weeks after that, you'll walk in on your husband fucking your co-worker, and your marriage will be over."

"Pregnant?"

"Yes."

"I don't get it."

"Steve needs to pay for the shit he's put you through. Without chopping his dick off, the only way to truly cause him pain is by hitting him where it counts."

"In his wallet," Marlene said.

I nodded. "Exactly."

Marlene covered her mouth with her hand. I sat back in my chair and sipped my Cosmo.

"Wow," Marlene said. "Wow . . . that's . . . that's . . . wow."

"For eighteen years you can make him pay, Marlene. The way you hate him now—he'll hate you every time he goes in his wallet."

"Wow," Marlene said again.

"Can you do it?"

"I . . . I don't know."

I drank my Cosmo down and stood up. "Like I said, let me know in four weeks. If you do, then we have a deal. If you don't, this conversation never happened. Go upstairs and get some rest. We have a big day tomorrow."

Without saying another word, I walked away, leaving Marlene alone with her thoughts.

On my way out, I stopped by the couple with the baby girl. I was standing beside the wife's shoulder, blocking the husband's view. "She's adorable," I said.

The mother, who was far more attractive than Anna Nicole's twin, smiled at me. "Thank you."

"What's her name?"

"Hailey."

"That's a pretty name. How many months is she?"

"Four and a half."

I smiled. "So precious," I said.

The woman smiled, thanked me again and kissed Hailey's cheek. I looked from the wife to the husband. He'd gone from focusing on the blonde's tits to mine. I cleared my throat, causing him to avert his gaze upward.

I smiled at him.

He smiled back.

"Your wife is much sexier than she is," I said.

Then I left.

Behind me, I heard his wife ask him what I'd meant by that. He stuttered and said he had no idea. In the mirror by the bar, I could see his wife turn around to look in my direction. I also saw her eyes stop dead on Anna Nicole's twin.

I smiled and went up to my room.

In Marlene's dreams that night, I was the woman being fucked by her husband.

6

Four weeks and three days later, Marlene walked into my office, closed the door and said, "I'm pregnant." I was sitting behind my desk going over some designs for XXXstacy's line. I put my pen down and looked at her. "Are you sure?" "Confirmed by my doctor." I nodded. "Did you tell Steve?" "Yes." "And his reaction?" "He's thrilled. He wants a boy." "And how are you? Are you thrilled?" Marlene smiled. "Actually, I am. I'm going to be a mommy." I smiled. "Congratulations."

Marlene smiled again and put her hand on her flat belly. It was too early for her to be glowing, but she was. I was about to switch topics and talk about work when she spoke first.

"So . . . two weeks, right?"

I looked up at her. "Two weeks?"

She gave a nod. "I held up my end of the deal."

"You still want to go through with it?"

"Of course. Why would you assume I wouldn't want to?"

"You just seem so happy. I assumed that you were going to stay with him."

Marlene shook her head and brushed her hand through her hair again. I wondered if she'd stop doing that after Steve was out of her life. "I told him I was pregnant three days ago. Last night, after a *late night* at work, he had pussy on his breath. I'm happy at becoming a mother. Remaining married to him is not an option. Now, are you backing out?"

I leaned back in my chair and folded my arms across my chest. "Why would you think I would back out?"

"Just making sure."

"The real question is, are you ready to pay half now?"

"My checkbook is in my office."

"Won't Steve notice the money missing?"

"I have a private account he knows nothing about."

"Then get your checkbook."

Ten minutes later, I was holding a check for twenty-five thousand dollars. It was the most money I'd ever held in my hand at one time. It was an electric feeling. Made me wonder how many more Marlenes were out there. How many more were that desperate? How many more were that fed up?

"So what's next?" Marlene asked. She was sitting on the opposite side of the desk, her legs crossed, her hands intertwined across her knee.

I folded the check in half and kept it tight between my fingers. "I want you to have a get together this weekend to celebrate the success of XXXstacy's line. Invite a large number of people. VPs, directors, assistants. Invite XXXstacy if you want. Make sure your house is packed. During the party, I'll plant the seeds for what is going to happen the following Friday."

"Next Friday?"

"Yes. You're still in bliss from finding out you're going to be a mommy, so you cut your business trip short to come home and be with your husband."

"Business trip?"

"Take a few days off starting next Wednesday. Tell Steve you have to go to Houston to meet with XXXstacy about the line. Take a mini-vacation somewhere. Go away with a friend or find a young stud and take him with you. Make sure you go someplace where there's no chance of running into family or friends."

"And while I'm away, you'll be . . ."

"Cultivating the seeds I've planted."

Marlene nodded.

I continued.

"At exactly nine-thirty that Friday night, you'll walk into your house with a friend that you had to call to pick you up from the airport since you couldn't reach Steve after you called him repeatedly. When you walk in, you'll find me riding Steve on your couch."

I stopped talking and looked at Marlene closely, looking for a reaction to what I'd just said. Would I see apprehension in her eyes? Would I see doubt? Regret, perhaps?

Her nightmares would become a reality. Love him or hate him, she'd be privileged to a front row seat to see that other woman in her dreams fucking her man. How would she take that? Could she handle it?

Seconds that seemed like minutes passed.

I watched her.

Her body language, her eyes—they told me the same thing: continue.

"I want you to go off on me. Go off on Steve. Wake the neighborhood. Give an Oscar-worthy performance. The next day, we'll meet and you'll give me the other half of the money. You'll be a free woman after that."

"Just like that?"

"Just like that."

Marlene smiled. "My family won't be able to say shit."

"No, they won't."

"I'll finally get to be the god damned victim."

"Finally."

"Wish I didn't have to wait two weeks."

"If you want the harvest, you have to give those seeds time."

Marlene said, "A lot of our fruits and vegetables are designed to grow in labs now."

I smiled. "I don't like lab grown fruits and vegetables."

"They say it's better for you."

"God designed fruits and vegetables to grow from the earth and from trees. How could they be better coming from a lab?"

"I don't know. They just say it is."

"We need to get our shit together and stop screwing up the earth. Then there'll be no need for fake foods."

"True."

"Go and plan that get together, Marlene. Blink, and two weeks will be here."

Marlene stood up and walked to the door and put her hand on the knob to pull it open. Funny, I thought. We were behind closed doors discussing the ruin of her marriage. I wondered what other business transactions people were discussing with their doors closed at that exact moment.

The door still not opened, Marlene turned to me. "Lisette, can I ask you something?"

"Of course."

"How long did it take you to come up with this plan?"

I folded the check in half again and laid it down on my desktop.

How long?

Back in Houston.

After our discussion.

After the couple with the baby.

In the room masturbating, imagining being fucked by the man who invented it.

That's where the plan came to fruition.

Funny thing was I never really gave it any thought.

My fingers worked me the way I imagined Steve's dick working me. Rotating clockwise. Counterclockwise. Back and forth. Fast. Slow. Hard. Soft.

I came.

The idea was born.

"Not long," I answered.

Marlene hmph'd and then opened the door and walked out.

I looked down at the twice-folded check. Twenty-five thousand dollars. It was addictive.

7

Marlene's house.

Packed.

People talking, drinking, laughing.

I was sitting on Marlene's leather sofa. My legs were crossed. A lot of skin was showing, thanks to the thigh-high, form-fitting, strapless black dress I had on. I'd bought it in Saks Fifth Avenue in Manhattan.

A mannequin was rocking the hell out of it. Rocking it so fierce that I didn't care about the price to lack of fabric ratio. I shelled out the money and then rocked it that night. Made a lot of heads turn. Made a lot of mouths drop.

Made a lot of females jealous.

This was the second time I'd worn it. Some people, when they find an outfit they like, they wear it every other week. Some forget about the other, and put it on every week. They usually have a favorite day.

That's not me.

I don't believe in over-wearing an item. I like to wear something, leave an impression and then let it sit. If you wear something too many times, the effect disappears. Once, twice, maybe three times I'll put an outfit on. After that, it goes to the back of the closet. For what I had in mind, Marlene's get together was the perfect occasion to rock it again.

I was holding a glass filled with champagne. Marlene had recently made a toast, thanking everyone, including herself, for all of the hard work on XXXstacy's line. In her speech, she said that she decided to throw the get together because she knew the big wigs weren't going to.

The whole time during her toast, my eyes had been on Steve, and his eyes had been on me. They had been on me since I'd walked into their mini-mansion. With our eyes, Steve and I flirted. Well, he flirted. I spun my web. Every chance she could, Marlene watched.

Steve was *GQ* sexy. White button-down shirt. No tie. Black slacks. Matching blazer. Staring at him, I thought about Marlene's statement again.

He fucks like he invented it.

Listening to Marlene's toast, smiling along with everyone else, staring into Steve's blue eyes, I had no doubt that her statement was true.

After making unimportant small talk with a few of my co-workers, I moved to the couch and continued to watch Steve as he played the loving husband role. Arm around Marlene's waist, smiling, chatting, laughing when it was required, and feigning interest when he had to.

He was good.

Occasionally I would look at Marlene and watch the subtle, disgusted expression appear on her face whenever Steve laughed or called her "Hon" out loud.

I sipped some champagne and watched Steve over the rim of my glass as he watched me. Seductively, I sent a message with my tongue as I licked my lips. Then I stood up, walked to the front door, opened it and stepped outside.

Five minutes later, the door opened behind me.

"Lisette?"

I turned around. "Steve."

"Are you all right?"

I nodded. "I'm fine. Why?"

"You left the party and came outside. I thought maybe something was wrong."

I shook my head. "No. I just needed some air. Besides, it's a little stuffy in there."

Steve smiled a sexy smile and stepped outside. "I know what you mean," he said, closing the door behind him. Before it closed completely, I saw Marlene staring in our direction.

I looked at Steve and smiled when the door closed. He smiled back, his smile giving me goose bumps, and said, "So, are you enjoying yourself?"

"I am. I just had to get away for a few minutes."

"I understand," Steve said, laughing slightly. "I try to avoid spending any more time with my co-workers than I have to also."

I wanted to say, "Except your secretary," but I didn't, and smiled instead.

"So, you guys really have great things going with this rapper."

"Yeah."

"Very stylish designs. I hear you're responsible for all of that."

I shrugged. "I've come up with a few designs."

"From what a lot of those co-workers inside say, without the designs you created, the line wouldn't be as successful."

I shook my head. "I just come up with designs. What's really made it a success has been all of the marketing. That's Marlene's area. She really deserves the credit. She's pretty phenomenal with the ad campaigns."

At the mention of his wife's name, Steve looked over his shoulder at the door. If he had x-ray vision, I have no doubt he would have used it at that very moment to see where she was. I didn't need superpowers to know she was practically leaning against the door with a cup against her ear.

"Shouldn't you be getting back inside?" I asked. "I'm sure Marlene misses you."

Steve shook his head. "She's entertaining. She probably doesn't even notice that I'm gone."

"I'm sure she notices."

"What makes you say that?"

"Because I'd notice."

And there it was. The bait.

Steve looked at me with hunger in his eyes.

I watched him with seduction in mine.

Laughter came from behind the door. Marlene's voice. First close. Then drifting away.

His eyes still on me, Steve said, "See . . . entertaining."

"I see."

Steve and I watched each other as a soothing, nighttime breeze blew around us. The temperature outside was around seventy-five degrees.

The gaze coming from Steve's blue eyes was much warmer. He looked me up and down, his eyes going from my breasts down to my legs, and back up again.

"Your hair looks nice pinned up like that."

"Thank you."

"You're a beautiful woman, Lisette."

I looked at him, but didn't say anything. I wanted him to keep going. I wanted to see how bold he would get.

"That dress . . . on you . . . wow. I've seen beautiful women before, but you . . . you're different."

"Different? Different how?"

"You're just different," he replied. "You have a sex appeal that's just damn infectious."

I raised an eyebrow. "Infectious?"

"Very."

"You're flirting with me."

"You were flirting with me inside."

"Was I?"

"Your lips . . . I saw you licking them."

"They were dry."

"A tongue doesn't move the way yours did to quench dry lips."

I took a step closer toward him. "And how did my tongue move?"

"Deliberately, like it was longing to lick something else."

I licked my lips for his benefit. "Hmmm."

Voices came from behind the door again. More laughter. The temperature in the air had risen by about twenty degrees. Steve was an ass and deserved what he had coming to him, but I won't lie . . . he was looking good and had me moist, thinking about Marlene's statement again.

I let my eyes drift downward and settle on a growing bulge in his pants. The bulge jumped once, twice. I looked back up at Steve.

I said, "Is that what you think? That I'm longing to lick something else?"

"I don't know. Are you?"

I took another step closer. We were standing inches apart now, our breath intertwining. If someone opened the door, they'd probably assume we'd been kissing. The sexual tension that hovered between us was thick. The excitement and audacity strong. I stared into Steve's eyes. He resembled a wolf, staring at prey. He wanted to pounce. He wanted to devour.

I licked my lips again. Then I put my hand on his crotch. Felt him throb. Felt him grow. I looked into his eyes as I held him.

He was gone.

If I told him to fuck me right then and there, he would have.

"Have you ever been with a black woman before, Steve?" I asked, wrapping my fingers around his girth. "Have you ever tasted one?"

Steve's manhood pulsed. "Never," he said.

"Would you like to know what it's like?" I grabbed hold of his hand and guided it to the bottom of my skirt. "Would you like to know how it feels?" He caressed the inside of my thigh. "Would you like to see how wet it is?"

As more laughter erupted inside of his house, Steve's hand slithered beneath my skirt and made its way upwards toward my shaved pussy.

I squeezed his crotch. Stroked it over his pants.

He sucked in a quick breath.

He was on the brink of explosion.

I tightened my grip around him and stroked him faster. "Would you like to fuck me, Steve?"

His breathing quickened even more.

His fingers were at my door, about to turn the knob and slide inside.

Before they could, I let go of him and stepped back.

Seconds later, the front door opened. Bill, from marketing, and his wife, Rita. Over Steve's breathing and between my questions, I'd heard them faintly telling everyone goodbye.

I smiled at Bill. As I did, Steve dug his hands in his pocket and pretended to be looking for something, while trying to adjust himself. Bill smiled back at me and walked by, oblivious.

His wife. When she walked by, she made eye contact with me and gave me a scowl.

A woman always knows.

When Bill and Rita were gone, I looked at Steve. He'd managed to regain his composure. I licked my lips and then without a word, walked by him and went back inside.

Marlene was waiting for me. Standing between the living and dining rooms, she watched me. I gave her a nod, and then went to get something to drink. I was sipping some champagne when Steve came inside, walked past me as though he hadn't almost finger-fucked me.

He went upstairs.

Was gone for a few minutes.

When he came back down, he had on a different pair of pants.

Marlene, who hadn't moved, saw that and looked at me.

I took another sip of my champagne then put the glass down, grabbed my purse from where I'd left it on the couch, and left.

8

Three days later.

Lunchtime.

Steve walked into my office and closed the door.

I looked up at him, not surprised to see him, but rather surprised that he hadn't come two days earlier. He'd cum in his pants, and I knew he was going to want to finish what I'd started. The way I'd teased and then left him; his dick might have grown limp after he came, but I know in his head, he was still rock hard. Men were weak like that.

I said, "Steve."

He said, "Lisette."

"Are you looking for Marlene?"

Steve walked up to my desk. "You know I'm not."

I closed my eyes a bit, then hit save on the report I'd been working on, and leaned back in my chair and folded my arms across my chest. "Do I?"

He leaned forward on my desk. "Is this some sort of game you're playing?"

"I don't play games, Steve."

Steve clenched his jaws. "This doesn't make sense." He paused and let out a frustrated breath.

"What doesn't?"

"Last Friday . . . what happened outside . . . what the hell was that about?" He clenched his jaws again.

I stared at him for a moment, watching his white face turn maroon. He was used to being in control and having it as well. I could tell by the tension in his posture and the frustration in his eyes that he'd never been in the position where he'd never had control from the beginning. And he most certainly had never lost it like he had when he ejaculated in his pants. "You never answered my question," I said.

"What question?"

My eyes on his, I said, "Do you want to fuck me?"

I watched him watch me. I could see the wheels in his brain spinning.

He said, "I thought you were Marlene's friend."

I stood up, walked around my desk, and stood in front of him. I was wearing a silk, lavender blouse and a black skirt that stopped in the middle of my thigh. No stockings. Just a thong underneath. "Do you plan on telling Marlene?"

He shook his head. "No."

"Then Marlene and I will still be friends."

Steve swallowed. Looked past me to the door. Then back at me. I glanced down and saw his crotch jump beneath his pants.

This was just too easy.

I leaned forward, brought my lips toward his, and dared him to move away with my eyes. "Answer my question, Steve," I said, my full lips centimeters away from his thin ones. "Do you want to fuck me?"

Steve's breathing was quick, shallow. I could practically hear his heart pulsating beneath his chest. I put my hand over his hard crotch.

He took in a breath and said, "Yes." He tried to kiss me, but I wouldn't allow it.

I backed up a step and stared at him. Watched the rise and fall of his chest. He liked to work out. His chest and shoulders were both broad. I imagined running my hands over his pecs. I said, "Would you like to fuck me right now?"

"Yes," he answered.

I felt like asking him if he'd jump off a bridge for me, just to hear him say yes again. He was that far gone. Instead I asked, "Would you like to taste me?"

"Yes."

I erased the step I'd taken back and licked his lips. "I'm wet, Steve. I'm dripping."

"I want to taste it," he said.

I stared at him as my body temperature rose. I was aroused. Extremely aroused. When I'd come from around my desk to stand in front of him, I'd only intended on getting him worked up the way I had before. I wanted to make him beg with his eyes. I wanted to tease him and leave him hanging again. But standing in front of him . . . feeling his erection . . . seeing the animalistic desire in his eyes . . . the control I had was total. The power was electric.

He wanted to taste me.

I wanted to make him taste me.

I said, "Eat me."

Steve stared at me, and then looked to the door again.

"Eat me now."

I moved from in front of him and went back to my chair and sat down. "Come and taste it," I said.

Steve flexed his jaws again.

He wanted to say no, that it was too dangerous.

He stared at my pussy.

He desperately wanted to say no.

But he couldn't.

He came and knelt down in front of me and
parted my legs with his hands.

I licked my lips and put my hands behind his
head and guided him downtown. I closed my
eyes and exhaled as his tongue slid inside of me.

Like an archeologist, Steve explored the walls
of my pussy, sweeping from side to side in swift,
seizure-like motions. Left. Right. Left. Right. I
exhaled and bit down on my bottom lip when his
tongue changed directions and moved up and
down.

I put more pressure on the back of his head.
Steve let out a low growl, audible to only us, and
spread my legs wider and drove his tongue deeper
inside of me.

I exhaled.

Got the chills.

The things he was doing to my clit.

I exhaled again.

My chills became shivers.

"Make me cum, Steve," I said, moving my hips. "Make . . . me . . . cum."

Steve licked, nibbled, sucked.

I moaned.

Shivered some more.

Then I pushed his face into me and suffocated him as I erupted. Made him lick and swallow until I was spent and then let go of his head.

Total control. The ultimate aphrodisiac.

Still on his knees, he looked up at me. "Did you enjoy that?" he asked.

I slid my skirt down and stared at him. Men. Always needing reassurance. Always needing to have their egos stroked.

I could have told him that, yes, I had enjoyed making him do what I wanted. That his weakness could bring out the freak in me. But he couldn't handle the truth.

I reached across my desk, picked up the phone, dialed an extension, and looked at him as I said into the receiver, "Hey, Marlene. You have a few minutes to go over some ideas I've come up with?"

Steve's eyes widened with surprise and disbelief. He stood up.

"Okay," I said. "Call me when you're finished."

I hung up the phone and stared at Steve. He called me a bitch with his eyes. I wanted to laugh.

I said, "Do you still want to fuck me?"

Steve flexed his jaws. He wanted to say no. He wanted to curse me out, maybe even hit me. His face was maroon again and going toward purple. I could see it in his eyes. He didn't want to deal with me and my bullshit anymore. He could go and get pussy somewhere else.

But it wouldn't be my pussy.

And after having knocked on the door and taken one step inside, I could also see in his eyes that he wanted to completely cross the threshold more than ever.

He said, "Marlene told me this morning that she has a business trip to go on. She leaves Wednesday. Are you going too?"

I shook my head. "No."

"Can I see you Saturday?"

"Friday," I said. "I have plans Saturday."

"Okay. Do you like Italian food?"

I shook my head. "This isn't a date, Steve. I'll be at your house between eight-thirty and nine."

"My house?"

"Your house," I said.

He opened his mouth to respond, but the ringing of my phone pierced the air before he could.

I looked at the caller ID, and then answered. "Hey, Marlene. Yes, now's a good time. Okay . . . I'll see you in five minutes." I put down the phone. "You better get going," I said, looking up at Steve. "Marlene won't wait five minutes."

He glared at me. He wanted to speak, but he knew he had no time. Completely frustrated, he turned and went to the door.

With his back to me, I said, "You may want to stop by the men's room on the way out and clean your face."

Without a reply, Steve opened the door and hurried out in the opposite direction from where Marlene would be coming. Two minutes later, after I picked up my thong and slipped it into my purse, Marlene walked into my office.

9

"Steve was just here."

Marlene stared at me. "Really?"

"Yes."

"What did he want?"

Bluntly, I answered, "Me."

Marlene hmph'd, passed her hand through her hair and said, "Fucking asshole."

"He ate my pussy," I said.

I watched her closely, looking for her reaction. I wanted to see how hearing something like that would affect her. Could she handle it? Could she deal with the picture her imagination would conjure up? If she could . . . if this wouldn't phase her, then Friday was still a go, which meant Saturday I'd be depositing another twenty-five thousand into my bank account. If she couldn't handle it, then there was no way she could deal with walking in and seeing me riding him. Of course, however she reacted would mean little to me. I already had half of the money in the bank that she was not getting back. I'd also had one hell of an orgasm.

Marlene looked at me, then looked off to the side and passed her hand through her hair again. "Unbelievable," she said. "He has absolutely no respect for me."

I raised an eyebrow. "None."

Marlene looked back at me. She asked, "Was it good?"

That actually shocked me. I wouldn't have expected a question like that to have come from her.

"It was," I said.

Marlene frowned. "But you would never have married him, right?"

I shook my head. "Never."

Marlene sighed. "I was just so damn frustrated. My exes—God, they couldn't perform. Do you know what it's like to not be satisfied?"

I shook my head again.

"After the first night with Steve, I just couldn't imagine putting myself in a position to be sexually frustrated again."

"So you and your pussy latched on to Steve."

"As if our lives depended on it, yes."

"And now look at you."

Marlene sighed again. "I know." She looked off to the side again and then back at me with pleading eyes. "Did he even hesitate before he . . . touched you?"

"No."

"Fucking asshole." She covered her face with her hand and began to cry softly.

I watched her and shook my head disdainfully. A woman crying over a man. I hated that. Hated to see a woman stress over a man's shortcomings. Especially when the woman had her shit together and didn't need the bastard.

"Why are you crying, Marlene?"

Marlene sniffled and then wiped tears away with her hands. "I'm sorry. I'm just frustrated and angry."

"Your tears are a waste of time."

"I know," Marlene said, looking down at the carpet.

"Men like Steve don't deserve your frustration or your anger."

"I know," she said again, the tone in her voice dejected.

I rolled my eyes. "Look at me, Marlene."

Marlene lifted her head. Her nose had started to change to a deeper shade of red from her crying. The flesh beneath her eyes was puffing up a bit.

"Marlene, in three days you're going to walk in your home and find your husband fucking your co-worker. You're going to have a friend with you to witness this. After Friday night, you will be able to divorce Steve without a hassle from your family or friends. Not only that, but Steve will be paying out of his ass in child support for the baby you're carrying." I paused, pressed my lips together tightly, and gave her a come-on-now look. "What the hell are you crying for? Steve's an ass. You know that. The fact that he would come here and eat my pussy shouldn't surprise you, and it damn sure shouldn't upset you. I mean, let's be real here. Are you or are you not paying me to trap your husband?"

Marlene nodded. "I am."

"All right, then. Did you think that I wouldn't do my job and do it well?" I gave her another look and didn't wait for her to answer. "Marlene, life is about to get a whole hell of a lot better for you. Just relax and let everything unfold. Save the tears for when you're laughing at Steve's pathetic ass."

Marlene gave a half smile and then stood up to leave.

"Marlene, before you go . . . did you get a boy toy to go away with?"

Marlene looked down at me. "I'm going away with my friend Jill. I'm pregnant. A boy toy just didn't seem right."

I gave her a nod and put my focus back on the report I was working on before Steve's appearance. I would have taken a boy toy.

10

Friday night.

Marlene's house.

Time to seal the deal.

I didn't realize it then, but my life was about to change forever.

I pressed the doorbell and waited for three minutes before Steve opened the door. He was wearing a white V-neck T-shirt that clung to his well-developed torso, and a pair of beige linen slacks. He was barefoot. He said, "Lisette."

I stared at him. He'd made me wait because he didn't want to seem anxious. But I knew he was. I could hear the excitement in the tone of his voice that he tried to keep calm and smooth. I could see it in his eyes. He couldn't wait to taste me again. He was dying to touch me, dying to slide inside of my pussy.

My black pussy.

Forbidden fruit he'd never had before.

He was so far gone. If I told him to get on his knees and crawl around while barking like a dog, he'd do it without hesitation. His eyes and body language told me that. It was amusingly sad how whipped he was.

I said, "Steve."

He stepped to the side. "Come in."

I stepped past him into the foyer and felt his eyes on me. I was wearing a striking, barely-there black dress I'd bought from Frederick's of Hollywood. Exposed, strappyback, butterfly detail; it fell mid-thigh, and had a six-inch slit on the side of my right leg. I bought it the day after he visited my office. Had it sent UPS overnight. Black pumps completed my ensemble. I turned around slowly, giving him an opportunity to admire what he would be emptying his pockets for eighteen years for.

He stared at me, shook his head and said, "Christ, you are a beautiful woman."

I said, "I'm a beautiful black woman."

"Yes, you are."

"Say it."

"You are a beautiful black woman."

I gave him a soft, sensual kiss on his cheek. "Good boy." And then I took a step back and fixed my eyes on him for a moment before dropping my gaze down to his crotch.

I thought about Marlene's statement again.

Thought about the way his tongue had made me explode.

I became moist with the thought.

I stretched my hand toward his crotch, grabbed his zipper, pulled it down, and let his manhood breathe. I looked down and stared at it. It wasn't the longest or the thickest I'd ever seen, but it was adequate.

I looked back up at Steve.

He looked at me.

Sex hovered around us, eager for things to unfold.

My eyes on Steve's, I wrapped my hand around his shaft and started to stroke him. I moved slowly at first, squeezing him every couple of seconds. Then I loosened my grip and stroked him faster. His body was tense. His breathing was quick.

I stroked.

Made him jerk.

Made him moan.

Made him say, "Shit."

I stroked.

Quickly at the tip.

Slowly down his shaft.

Steve said, "Shit," again.

He was almost there.

I was walking him, dick in hand, toward the point of no return.

"Do you have condoms, Steve?"

He moaned, said, "Shit," again, and then, "I . . . in my pocket."

I let go of him and said, "I'm thirsty."

Steve looked at me and smiled. "I didn't think you swallowed."

My eyes became slits. "I want water."

Steve's smiled disappeared. "Water?"

I took a step back. "With ice." I moved away from him and headed to the living room.

Steve didn't move for a few seconds. A few more strokes and he would have been there. But I couldn't have that.

I turned and looked at him over my shoulder. "Is something wrong, Steve?"

He put his manhood away and turned around. He shook his head. "No."

He was so irritated, I wanted to laugh. "Not too much ice," I said.

I went into the living room and sat down on their sofa. Dark brown Italian leather. Cool and soft. I leaned back against the down-blended cushions and inhaled the hardly-ever-used fragrance it gave off. I smiled to myself. In a few minutes it wasn't going to be cool, and it damn sure was going to give off a different fragrance.

I looked around the living room; something I hadn't really done when I was there last. A matching recliner sat off to the right side, an accent chair to the left. The coffee and side tables were made from dark cherry wood and had marble tops. Their entertainment center was dark cherry also, and had antique-style brass-finished hardware. A fifty-inch plasma television set sat in the middle. A cable box, DVD player, and Bose stereo components sat on shelves at the bottom. Matching left and right tier units were filled with books, ranging from encyclopedias to Shakespeare to James Patterson, along with small decorative vases and bowls. The walls were beige, the hardwood floor dark. A painting of either Marlene's or Steve's grandmother hung over a fireplace set against the far wall. Another painting of what looked to be a Van Gogh hung near the entertainment unit. With the exception of the portrait of Grandma, there were no other pictures of family anywhere. I couldn't help but wonder if Grandma wasn't Grandma at all, but rather just some random picture picked to take up empty space. The room was cold and lifeless. It was Marlene's marriage.

Steve came into the living room with my water. "Here you go."

I took it, sipped a little, and then handed it back to him. "Thank you."

Bewilderment crept onto Steve's face. "Is something wrong with the water?"

I shook my head. "No. Why?"

"You only took one sip."

"That's all I wanted."

"But . . . I thought you were thirsty."

"I was. Now I'm not."

Steve set the glass down by the entertainment center, exhaled and put his left hand on the back of his neck and squeezed.

"Something wrong?" I asked.

Steve shook his head, but didn't say anything right away. I observed his body language. He was tired of me. He was fed up with the game. He could have been fucking his secretary at that very moment.

I took a discreet look at the time displayed on the cable box: 9:00.

Thirty minutes was all I'd need.

I stepped toward him. "You seem irritated."

Steve shook his head. "No. I'm just—"

"Do you want me to leave?" I said, putting my hand against his chest.

Steve looked down at my hand and then at me. He said, "No."

I licked my lips and traced my hand down his chest to his crotch again. "Do you still want me?"

"You know I do."

I leaned forward, carrying my lips up inches away from his. I gave his penis a squeeze and felt him grow hard instantly. Just like before, I pulled his zipper down and released him again. But I didn't stroke. I took a few steps back and said, "Take off your shirt."

Steve complied and removed his shirt, exposing a sculpted, hairless chest. I let my fingers roam over his pecs and then his abs for a moment before saying, "Take off the rest now."

He did as told. I let my eyes roam over the rest of him. Some people go to the gym to firm up their loose ends. Some go to look at the opposite sex and socialize. His arms, his chest, his abdominals, his legs; Steve went to the gym seeking only perfection.

I admired his physique and his rock-hard erection for a few seconds, and then reached for the button holding my dress up behind my neck. I undid it and let the dress fall down around my ankles. "Is this what you want, Steve?"

Steve's dick jumped at my complete nakedness. He answered, "Yes," and then took a step toward me.

I shook my head. "Stay."

Remaining in his place, Steve watched me as I took my hands from my neck to my breasts. I ran my fingers over and around them. I pinched my swollen nipples. I cupped my right breast and brought it up to my tongue and did slow circles around the nipple before taking my entire breast into my mouth. My eyes never left Steve the entire time.

I watched him watching me.

I watched his mouth fall open.

I watched his dick jump with each revolution my fingers and tongue made.

I watched the rise and fall of his chest quicken.

I watched him wrap his fingers around his shaft.

I caressed my breasts and watched him stroke.

I dropped my hand down to my very wet pussy, and tickled, tapped and two-fingered it. Then I pulled my fingers out and tasted my own sweetness. The pace of Steve's stroking increased after that.

My eyes went to the clock. 9:10.

"Get the condom, Steve." I moved back to the couch. "Put it on and come fuck me."

Steve let go of himself, bent down to his slacks, and pulled one out from his pocket. He was an animal as he tore it open, removed the latex, and rolled it down over himself. His eyes were ravenous. He meant business. He was going to show me that Marlene's words were the absolute truth.

I lay back on the couch and opened my legs. Like a lion pouncing on his prey, Steve was on top of me seconds later. He slid between my drenched walls and moved rhythmically. Back and forth. Clockwise. Counter-clockwise.

"You . . . feel . . . so . . . good, Lisette. You're so . . . so . . . wet. So tight."

I moaned. Got the chills. "Give it to me," I said. I tightened my walls around him.

He thrust harder, deeper.

My turn to say, "Shit . . . shit . . . shit . . . shit." I closed my eyes, collapsed my legs around his waist, lifted my hips, and took all he was giving me.

"Tell me you like it, Lisette. Tell me how good it feels."

I opened my eyes. Steve was looking down at me with a smile.

Damn.

I took a look at the time. 9:23. I pushed up on his chest and said, "Sit down."

Disappointment appeared in his eyes. For a moment he'd had control. He wanted to hear me tell him that he was the man. That he was fucking me like I'd never been fucked before. But that wasn't going to happen.

I pushed up on his chest again. "Sit."

He did.

My pussy was pulsating with excitement as I mounted him. The moment was nearing and I wanted to cum when that moment came. I moved my hips and took him deeper. He reached up to fondle my breasts. I wrapped my hands around his forearms and pushed them back against the couch, and kept them pinned there.

Marlene had said that he fucked like he invented it. A few minutes ago, I would have known whether or not that was true. A few minutes ago, I'd lost myself and had given up control. Now I had it back, and I'd never know if what she'd said was the truth because now I was fucking him. I dug my nails into his arms and made him moan.

I looked over my shoulder as I pounded him.

9:27.

I looked back at Steve. I wanted to look into his eyes when his world would be fucked up. I counted down the remaining minutes in my head.

At 9:28, my walls were on fire.

At 9:29, my pussy screamed.

At 9:30, I heard, "Oh my God!" And then a tidal wave exploded from inside of me.

Steve's eyes grew wide and his mouth fell open as Marlene screamed, "Oh my God!" again.

I drove my hips down on Steve one more time before he pushed me off of him. "Marlene!" He rushed to grab his clothing.

"You son of a bitch!" Marlene screamed. "You son of a bitch!"

I turned around on the now very wet sofa and faced Marlene. Her friend was standing beside her, shocked and dumbfounded. Marlene and I gave one another a look, and then she pointed at me.

"You?" She threw her hands over her mouth. "How could you?"

She was so good I wanted to smile.

I joined the act, covered myself with my hands and said, "Marlene . . . I . . . I'm so sorry."

"Sorry? Sorry? You bitch! I thought we were friends!"

His pants on but not buttoned, his shirt clutched in his hand, Steve pleaded, "Marlene . . . please . . . it's not . . . it's not . . . shit . . . I thought you weren't coming home until Sunday!"

The look on Marlene's face when she looked in his direction gave me the chills. She charged at him. "I hate you!" She swung out wildly and administered a slap across his cheek the neighbors two houses down probably heard. The neighbors three houses down probably heard the next one.

"I hate you!" Marlene screamed again, going on true, raw, pent-up emotion. "I fucking hate you!"

Steve backed away from Marlene and looked from Marlene to me to her friend. Shaking his head, he said, "Jill . . . this . . . this . . ."

Jill put up her hand. "Save it, asshole." She went over to Marlene, who was crying hard tears now, and put her hands around her shoulders. She consoled her, told her everything would be okay. Then she scowled at me. "I think you should leave."

I kept playing my part. "Marlene," I said, getting up from the couch and grabbing my dress. "I'm so sorry. I never meant . . . it . . . it just happened."

Marlene looked at me. Again we gave one another a look. She said, "I can't believe you would do this to me. We work together. We were friends."

"I'm so sorry," I said, slipping on my dress. "This was just a mistake. A terrible mistake. We are friends."

"You bitch! Don't you dare call us friends! Bitch! I should kill you!" She tried to charge at me, but Jill held her back.

"Marlene, don't! She's not worth it. He's not worth it!" Jill looked at me. "Leave. Now!"

I gave her a you-don't-know-who-you're-fucking-with look. I know she didn't have a clue and was just being a friend, but I still didn't like being talked to that way. I cut my eyes at her one more time, and then looked at Marlene. She was still glaring at me. I have to say, I was impressed. "I'm sorry," I said again. Then I hurried past them.

When I got to the front door, I heard something shatter. I paused with my hand on the knob and listened.

"You piece of shit! It's over! Get your things and get out now!"

"Marlene . . . please! I know I messed up, but we can work past this."

"Fuck you!"

Something else shattered.

Steve grunted and yelled out, "Shit! You cut me!"

I smiled, turned the knob and walked out.

The next day, I collected the other half of my money. This was supposed to have been a one time thing for me.

It wasn't.

11

One week later, I was working as a head designer for a different fashion company.

In order for everything to go smoothly for Marlene, she and I had to end our friendship. I was the other woman and there was just no way for me to stay on at LeVor without both of us having to constantly put on an act. She would have had to hate me. I would have had to continue to be apologetic. The men in the office would have looked at me with sinful intentions. I would have been a tramp in the women's eyes. I left LeVor for two reasons. One: I'd lowered myself and played the role with Marlene once, and I had no intention of doing it again. Two: I damn sure wasn't going to be disrespected by anyone at work.

Decision made, I bounced.

Fucked up Steve's world on Friday.

Collected the rest of my money from Marlene on Saturday.

Went to the office on Sunday to get the few personal belongings I had there.

Monday, I made a call to one of LeVor's rivals and took them up on an offer they'd made to me a month prior.

By Tuesday I had my corner office overlooking the city.

Three months after that, a woman I'd never met before was knocking on the front door of my condo.

I'd just come back from the gym. It was my kick boxing night. A few years back, I'd seen Jennifer Lopez's movie *Enough*. She portrayed an abused wife who faked her own death and then assumed a brand new identity. Her new life was good for her until her husband found out she was still alive. With her secret identity no longer a secret,

J. Lo had finally had enough. She took self defense classes, stopped being the hunted, and kicked some serious ass. I started taking kick boxing a week after that. Now I taught a class every Wednesday night. Needless to say, I was tired, sweaty, and starving.

I walked to the door, keys in hand, and looked at the woman, who stepped aside to make room. "Can I help you?"

The woman smiled. "Lisette, right?" she said with a Southern twang.

I stared at her. She knew my name. Instead of answering her question, I said, "And you are . . .?"

She put out her hand. "Sorry. I'm Lisa."

I looked at her hand, but didn't take it. "Lisa. Have we met?"

Lisa shook her head. "No."

I took a step back, balled my fists, and got into a fighting stance. Lisa and I had never met, yet she was standing at my front door. If I had to go J. Lo on her ass, I would.

Lisa put her hands up and said, "Whoa."

"How the fuck do you know my name? And what the fuck are you doing here?"

Lisa's eyes were wide. "We have a mutual friend."

"Friend? Who?"

"Marlene."

I jerked my head back slightly. Marlene. I hadn't seen her since she'd given me the other half of the money she owed me. We'd only spoken once after that. A short phone conversation.

She wanted to thank me again for what I'd done. She called a few times after that, but I never answered. Eventually she got the hint and stopped calling. "Marlene?"

Lisa nodded. "Yes."

I watched her closely. Studied her eyes, her body language. Tried to figure her out. Ultimately I couldn't, so I asked again, "What are you doing here?"

"Marlene sent me."

I raised an eyebrow. "She did?"

"Yes."

"Why?"

Lisa looked over my shoulder, down the hall, and then took a quick glance behind her. Satisfied that we were alone, she leaned forward a bit, and in a subdued tone, said, "She said you could help me."

I let go of some of the tension in my muscles and unclenched my fists. "Excuse me?"

"She said you could help me," Lisa repeated.

"I can?"

"Yes."

"And just how can I do that?"

Again she looked up and down the hallway. "She said you can help me divorce my husband."

I don't know if it's that I'm a cynic or a real-
ist, but very few things really shock the hell out
of me. A kid comes back to kick his high school
bully's ass, and kills him in the process—that's
real to me. A Catholic priest fucking around
with little boys because he's not allowed to do
what comes naturally with a woman, is sick, but
that's real to me. Women wanting to trap their
husbands is real to me. Marlene telling anyone
about what I'd done for her. Now, that shocked
me.

I looked at Lisa intently. There was desperation in her eyes, similar to what had been in
Marlene's back in Houston. I shook my head.
"I'm sorry, but I have no idea what you're talking
about."

Before I realized it was happening, Lisa stepped
forward and grabbed hold of my wrist. "Please!"
she said, her tone laced with the same desperation
as her eyes. "My husband beats the shit out me."

I looked at her hand clasped around my wrist
and then I looked up at her. "Let go," I said.

She did. "I'm sorry. I just . . ." She paused, let
out a labored breath. "I'm sorry," she said again.

My eyes on her, I rubbed my wrist and flexed
it. Fear and extreme anxiety had given her a

good amount of strength. "I can't help you," I said. "Call the police."

Lisa let out a chuckle. "My husband is the police. Captain of the hundred ninety-third precinct. Loved and respected by all. Some even want him to run for mayor."

I looked at Lisa. Stress had her eyes red with pain, with disappointment. Tears welled in the corners. He was the police. Damn.

I asked, "How old are you, Lisa?"

"Forty."

I shook my head. A grown woman living a lie. Sad. "I can't help you," I said again.

Lisa's shoulders slumped down. "Please," she said, her voice just above a whisper. "I . . . I have money."

"I'm sorry," I said. "But I can't help you."

Tears fell from her eyes down her cheeks. "But . . . Marlene said—"

"Marlene was mistaken." That said, I unlocked my door and left Lisa alone in the hallway, where she cried hard tears for a few minutes before shuffling away.

Two minutes after that, I called Marlene.

"Lisa was just here," I said when she answered. My voice was bitter. I was furious. "Why the fuck was she just here?"

Marlene responded with silence for a moment before saying, "Lisette . . . I . . . I'm sorry."

"I did you a favor, Marlene. From our lips to God's ears. It was supposed to stay that way."

"I know."

"Then why the fuck was Lisa here?" I asked again.

Marlene sighed. "Lisette . . ."

"Marlene."

"Lisa . . . I've known her for a long time. Since college. She's a good woman with a good heart. She was fooled. She thought she'd hit the jackpot with Brad. He was a rising star on the police force. He played the role better than Steve did. For five years, we all thought she was living the fairy tale life. Nice home, beautiful kids, a loving, caring husband that would and did do anything for her. I couldn't believe it when she told me. There was just no way the Brad I had come to know would ever put his hands on her. But then she showed me bruises."

"Marlene . . ." I started before being cut off.

"Lisette, what you did for me . . . it changed my life. I was unhappy. I was beaten emotionally. I was dying slowly each day, forcing myself to live a lie because I was just too afraid to say fuck everyone else. I know I was never supposed to tell anyone about what we did, but, Lisette . . . Lisa needs you."

"I did a favor for you, Marlene. I'm not a savior."

"You're wrong, Lisette. You are a savior. You saved me. Gave me strength I didn't know I had. You gave me a new life. Lisa . . . she's going to die if you don't help her."

I squeezed my eyes shut tightly. I didn't want to care. I didn't want Marlene's words to affect me. But I would have had to have been inhuman. "There's got to be someone she can go to for help."

"He's an extremely well-respected captain on the police force, Lisette. No one is going to believe that he beats his wife. And even if someone did, they wouldn't dare speak out against him."

"Why doesn't she just run away?"

"Brad's a public figure. There is no running away for her. Not without the media getting wind of this."

"That wouldn't be a bad thing."

"It was a struggle for her to open up to me, Lisette. She's a very proud woman. She doesn't want anyone knowing about this."

"There's got to be someone," I said again.

"Lisette, you don't have to sleep with him. Just trap him. Give Lisa something concrete that she can use that would give her the freedom she needs and deserves."

I shook my head. Again I said, "I'm not a savior."

"Please, Lisette. She's my friend and she's suffering, emotionally more than physically. Please help her. I'm begging you."

I shook my head again and gritted my teeth. I thought about Lisa and the look in her eyes. I thought about the way she'd grabbed my wrist. I remembered the strength in her cries outside of my door before she left. Marlene said she was going to die if I didn't help her. I couldn't help but wonder if my rejection hadn't already sent her on her way. Damn it, I didn't want to give a damn.

"Please, Lisette," Marlene pleaded again. "She's willing to pay you thirty thousand dollars."

"I don't need the money."

"That's bullshit, Lisette. Everyone needs money."

"Marlene—"

"I'll add another twenty to that. That's another fifty thousand dollars. And like I said, you don't have to sleep with him."

Another fifty thousand.

Like I said, I wasn't inhuman. And my being human made the prospect of getting another fifty thousand dollars extremely appealing.

Fifty thousand dollars.

Brad. He was another Steve, only worse.

Fifty thousand dollars.

I didn't have to sleep with him.

Fifty thousand dollars.

All I had to do was trap him. Give Lisa something she could use to bring him down.

Fifty thousand dollars.

He deserved to be trapped. Deserved to pay in whatever way Lisa wanted to make him pay. Lisa. For all of the shit she was enduring, she deserved it too. Helping her wouldn't put an end to the physical abuse of women, but it would put an end to hers. Like I said, I didn't want to care. Didn't want to give a shit.

But I did. And I won't lie; it had been an intoxicating feeling looking at the balance of my bank account after my night with Steve.

Fifty thousand dollars.

I was standing in front of my dressing table staring at myself in the mirror when I said, "Lisa left about thirty minutes ago. Call her and tell her to come back."

Marlene exhaled into the receiver. "Thank you, Lisette."

Three weeks later, I gave Lisa a videotape of her husband on all fours, barking like a dog, begging me to fuck him up his ass with a dildo he'd brought. Turns out, Captain Bradley Stern enjoyed a good, stiff dick as much as any woman did.

Weeks after that, I was sitting with Marlene in the small café at Barnes and Noble. She'd called me and asked me to meet her there. She said she was craving a Barnes and Noble turkey sandwich and a caramel macchiato. She also said she had something important to discuss with me. Something life-changing. I agreed to meet her only because she wouldn't take no for an answer. This was after Lisa and her bi-sexual captain of the police, who, by the way, had practically dropped off the face of the earth after Lisa made his secret known.

I was sipping on a vanilla latte, grande size, without whipped cream. She was drinking her macchiato with a lot of whipped cream. She'd devoured her sandwich seconds after she'd gotten it.

She was in her sixth month of pregnancy. For some women, pregnancy stole their beauty away. For others, it enhanced it. Marlene was in that percentile. Pregnancy was good to her. With the exception of a few additional pounds and a slightly wider nose, she was all belly. She was having a boy, and she was ecstatic.

"I know so many other Lisas, Lisette," she said. "I have so many other friends as fed up as I was. Paying money to get the results you can get for them wouldn't be an issue. I know women that can and would pay more than fifty thousand dollars."

She paused and looked at me. I kept silent, sipped my latte and waited to see where she was going.

"Become a private investigator, Lisette. You can insure yourself and your services. Someone doesn't like the results you provide—tough. Make them sign a contract. There wouldn't be a damn thing they could do."

I took another sip of my flavored coffee and said, "When did you come up with this idea?"

"After Lisa, I realized I had so many other friends that would be willing to pay for the same result."

"Willing to pay me?"

"Yes."

"What makes you so sure of that?"

"Once Benjamin is born, I'll be getting monthly checks from Steve for at least eighteen years. Lisa is now enjoying life and being fucked by one of her husband's former subordinates. The proof is in the pudding, Lisette, and as Steve found out, your pudding is gold."

I couldn't help it; I smiled.

"Lisette, I can bring clientele to you. You can make a lot of money. Easy money. And don't say you don't need or want it."

My eyes on hers, I took another sip of latte. She was a different woman from the one I'd sat in front of back in Houston. And it had nothing to do with the pregnancy. That Marlene had been a shell of a woman. She had a slumped, defeated posture. Stress lines decorated the corners of her eyes and mouth, and made her appearance synonymous with her broken spirit. The Marlene sitting before me, taking a sip of her heavily whipped-creamed caramel macchiato was the complete opposite. Shoulders pinned back and high, back arched, attitude laced with a confidence that made me feel as though, were she twenty years younger, she would have kept the clients all to herself.

"What do you get out of this, Marlene?"

"Satisfaction."

"Of?"

"Of seeing another woman liberated from the shit men put us through."

I closed my eyes a bit. "Satisfaction?"

Marlene said, "Yes." Then she cleared her throat and said, "And twenty percent."

Again I couldn't help it; I smiled again.

This was definitely not the same Marlene.

I said, "Twenty percent?"

"We can make a lot of money, Lisette. More importantly, we can do something that women have wanted to do to men for years—truly stick it to them."

"And you want twenty percent?"

"You know I have rich friends, Lisette. Twenty percent is nothing."

"Twenty percent of fifty thousand thousand leaves me with forty thousand."

"Forty thousand for what—three weeks' worth of work, tops? Hell, considering some of the assholes my friends are married to, in three weeks' time, you could have five or six clients."

"More."

Marlene smiled now. "I know. I was being conservative."

I gave Marlene a nod and sipped some more of my latte, which had become annoyingly lukewarm. Unless you rushed to drink it down, there was no sitting and taking the time to enjoy a hot beverage anymore. It was all a scam. Companies used cheaper paper cups. The drinks got colder faster. Consumers addicted to their tea, hot chocolate or java, had no choice but to spend another three dollars and change looking for the satisfaction they craved. Three dollars and change multiplied by two for every person, multiplied by more than a million people, was a hell of a lot of money for companies to recoup.

I took one last annoyed sip and then moved the cup to the side. There'd be no other drink for me. To hell with Barnes and Noble.

I looked at Marlene with a scrutinizing eye. "So you want to be my pimp, Marlene?"

Marlene's eyes widened. "No!"

"Offering out my services to paying customers . . . taking your cut . . . sounds like pimpin' to me."

Marlene shook her head vigorously. "No. That's not what I'd be doing at all."

I raised my eyebrows and said, "Really?"

"Really." Marlene's forehead knotted up as she grabbed her coffee and took a hard sip.

I held back a smile. I enjoyed putting her on edge.

Marlene put her cup down and passed her hands through her hair, which was a lighter shade of blonde now. "Lisette, in no way, shape or form is what I'm talking about to be confused with prostitution. Whether women like to admit it or not, men always have the upper hand. They can and have always been able to do what they want, when they want, with whomever they want." She lowered her voice a notch and leaned forward in her chair. "I'm talking about uprooting the playing field by giving women the opportunity to make the game backfire on the men. Or in some cases, instead of uprooting it, just leveling it by giving them something to hold over their asshole husbands' heads, so that they could do as the men have done."

"Like fuck the gardener or the mailman."

"And unless the husbands want their infidelity exposed—"

"They wouldn't say shit."

"Exactly."

I looked at Marlene and again thought about the woman back in Houston. She'd been so different. She'd been so weak. Now look at her. Lisa had been different too. She was an emotional wreck, beaten down and scarred. Now she was fucking a man that used to report to her ex-husband.

Uproot or level the playing field. It would be up to the woman to decide which option they wanted to go with. All I had to do was make it happen. And, according to Marlene, all she had to do was enroll her friends in the program. It's funny, but I should have been the one to come up with the plan.

I said, "Fifteen percent."

Marlene looked at me. Her eyes said that wasn't a fair deal at all.

Her plan, but, "I can get clients without you, Marlene." My tone was no-nonsense.

Marlene looked from me to her cup of macchiato, and then down to the floor.

Fifteen percent.

Take it or leave it.

Her choice.

A few seconds passed before Marlene looked at me again. Her eyes were saying something different this time. "Okay. Fifteen percent."

Present

12

Two years. That's how long I'd been a home wrecker.

Two years, six women empowered in one way or another. Marlene had friends. Her friends had friends. Her friends' friends had friends. Six degrees of separation. My clients and their reasons for needing and wanting my services varied. I had women like Lisa, either battered emotionally, physically, or both, who needed help escaping from the hell their bastards were putting them through. I felt sorry for these clients, but at the same time, they really annoyed the hell out of me with their teary sob stories, because I just couldn't understand taking a man's bullshit the way they did. A man had one opportunity with me. One disrespectful statement from his mouth. One violent physical outburst against me. That's all it would take for me to send the son of a bitch's balls up into his throat. I was and never would be the one, and I never will understand the women who do become the one.

Right or wrong, my fee was high for these clients.

I had other clientele who hired me to satisfy their nagging suspicions that their husbands weren't as faithful as they claimed to be. These clients usually hired me with the hopes that their husband's actions or lack of action toward me would prove that their men weren't typical. That was never the case. These clients always broke down after I presented them with evidence. These women made my head shake. They never understood that they were better off not knowing at all.

Then there were other Marlenes, who wanted hard evidence in one form or another to use against their husbands in court. Women fed up, who wanted to take their men to the cleaners. I respected these women.

Finally, there were the wives who didn't want a divorce. These were my favorites. I called them the lost and found. At one point, they'd lost their way by losing their control, but they'd found their way again when they realized that, short of literally dragging a man around by his dick, having evidence to hold over his bastard head was the best form of control any woman could have. These women got it. I charged them the most, because with the evidence in their hands, they could get anything they wanted.

Two years. Over three hundred thousand tax-free dollars earned. I'd kept my nine-to-five to keep Uncle Sam from asking questions.

Six women had finally grown tired of being humiliated and had come calling when all else had failed. They all wanted their dignity and control back. Control over their lives, control over the men that were fucking them up emotionally, physically, and spiritually. Marlene's friends.

Her friends' friends. Marlene may have been, but I wasn't on any type of moral crusade, although I will admit that it did feel good giving the women the upper hand. But like I said, it was all about the Benjamins for me. And my quest to get paid nearly got me killed.

13

Kyra Rogers. She would become my nightmare.

I was at work coming up with some new designs for a new client the company had taken on, when my silver Sidekick started vibrating. I had two Sidekicks, a black one and a silver one. Black was for everyday use. The silver rang only when my services were needed. It was two o'clock in the afternoon. My silver Sidekick was never supposed to ring until after five. These were the instructions I'd given to Marlene to give to any potential client. Prior to that day, every potential had followed protocol.

Kyra Rogers.

My Sidekick was top of the line, with a lot of features and capabilities I didn't utilize. Too bad it didn't have the capability to do a personality assessment for each caller. Had it been able to do that, I could have avoided the life-changing drama I would endure.

For a split second, I contemplated letting the call go to my voice mail, but I'd just recently eaten lunch, and my eyes were getting heavy. I needed the break. I answered the call.

"Hello."

"I want my husband trapped. Can you get the job done?"

Something about the tone in her voice didn't sit well with me. My gut was telling me to disconnect the call. Instead of listening, I said, "And you are?"

"Who I am only matters if you can get the job done."

I pulled my Sidekick away from my ear and gave it a who-the-fuck-is-this-bitch glare. I put it back to my ear and ignored the insistence from my gut.

"So can you or can't you?"

I sat up in my chair. We'd only been talking for a few seconds, yet for the first time, I felt as though I had no control. I didn't like the feeling at all. It was uncomfortable. I thought again about pressing for a name, but changed my mind. She knew who I was. I knew what she needed.

It was time to take my control back.

"And how much are you willing to pay for the results?"

Supply and demand. I had the supplies. My services were in demand. How desperate was she?

She said, "More than anyone has paid you before."

Her comment was direct and arrogant.

"And how would you know what I've been paid?"

"Believe me . . . I know."

My skin tingled as I fell back into that uncomfortable space again. Who the fuck was this woman? What exactly did she know?

Control.

Once again I didn't have it.

I looked at the clock on my PC, and once again ignored my instinct. More than anyone had paid me before. The statement was bold, loud, intriguing, scary and exciting all at the same time.

I asked again, "How much?"

She said, "Two hundred thousand dollars."

My heart started pop-locking beneath my chest.

Two hundred thousand dollars. Without question, more than anyone had paid me by far.

"What has he done? Or what is he doing?"

"Nothing."

I raised an eyebrow. "Nothing?"

"Nothing."

"And you want to pay me two hundred thousand dollars to trap him?"

"Yes."

I was silent for a moment. Like I said before, I'd taken on the clients not because I was on any type of moral crusade, but rather because they were paying me large sums of money. Having said that, each one of my clients' husbands had deserved what he'd gotten.

The scales have never been balanced when it comes to the battle of the sexes. Men have always been able to play the field the way they see fit. I was doing what I was doing for the money, yes, but there was a part of me that was enjoying it and taking some pride in the fact that for once, the scales had been tipped the other way.

I'd never taken down a man that didn't deserve it, but I'd never been offered that kind of money in one shot before.

I said, "Two hundred thousand dollars?"

"Yes."

"Your husband hasn't done anything and isn't doing anything, but you want to pay me to set him up. Why?"

"I'm offering more money than anyone's paid you before. I can take it somewhere else, you know."

"If that were true, you wouldn't have called me."

Seconds of silence was her response.

What I'd said had been the absolute truth. She'd called me because there was no one else that could do what I did. That's what she'd heard from any other clients she may have spoken to. That's what she'd heard from Marlene, if Marlene was that person. I was worth every penny, because I was the best.

She exhaled. "My husband is a rich man. He gives me anything I want. He treats me like a queen, never disrespecting me in any way, shape or form."

An incoming e-mail popped up on my screen. A message from the head of the company. Something about the company and its focus on diversity. I deleted it and said, "So what's the problem?"

A sigh. "He's killing me."

"Killing you?"

"Yes. Every damn day, I'm dying from boredom."

"So take up a hobby."

"I don't want or need a hobby. What I need is to get out of this god-damned fairy tale."

"Does your husband sleep around with other women?"

"No. But God, I wish he did. I wouldn't have needed to call you."

"How do you know he's not?"

"I've tried setting him up before. I've paid hookers—good looking, stunning ones, to seduce him."

"And he's never given in to them?"

"Not even once."

"So he's turned down the high-priced ho's. What about the women you haven't paid?"

She chuckled again. "What women? I've had him followed daily for the past four months, hoping to catch him doing something. Do you want to know what his daily routine is?" She didn't wait for a response. "At six in the morning he goes to the gym, where he proceeds to keep to himself and work out. At seven-thirty, he's off to Starbucks to have a morning cup of coffee and work on his laptop for a few. He never once flirts with the attractive twenty-something female behind the counter who practically drools over him every time he comes in. At eight-thirty he heads to the office, where he does nothing but work.

"For lunch, he eats whatever meal he's packed the night before. If he's not eating something he's packed, then he's out with a client, conducting business. And not business in quotation marks. He stays at work until eight, nine o'clock, leaves the office, and makes a pit-stop at Starbucks for his nightly java fix. The twenty-something girl from the morning is gone, but there's another twenty-something hoping to be noticed, that he ignores just the same. After his coffee, he comes home, gives me a peck on my cheek, and then heads into his study to continue working.

"That's his daily routine. So to answer your question . . . there aren't any other women aside from the high priced hoes."

"What about other men?"

"What about them?"

"Could he be on the down low?" I asked, thinking back to Lisa and her ex-captain.

"No chance."

"How do you know? Ever tried to test him that way?"

"Yes. And the end result was a threat to the guy I'd paid to get the fuck away from him before he killed him."

I nodded, sent another meaningless e-mail—this one from DeDe in H.R.—to the trash. "Are you sleeping around?" I asked. I knew the answer already, but I asked anyway.

"I have."

I shook my head and leaned back in my chair, wondering just who the hell Marlene had sent my way and why.

"What's your name?"

"Does it really matter?"

I closed my eyes a fraction and thought about her question. Then I said, "No, it doesn't. Find somebody else. I can't help you." And then I disconnected the call.

Fifteen seconds later, my silver Sidekick vibrated again. I let it vibrate a few times, and then answered. "Yes."

"Have you ever seen the movie *Hitch*, Lisette?"

First time she'd used my name. I didn't like the way it sounded coming from her. *Hitch*. I'd seen the movie many times. Drooled over Will Smith and swore Jada wasn't good enough every time I saw it. I didn't know where she was going with the question. Something told me I didn't want to know. I said, "I have."

"Do you remember when his occupation was outed? Do you remember what happened?"

Things crumbled for my man, that's what happened. He lost his job, he lost friends, and he lost respect. He did get the girl in the end, though, but that was only because it was a movie. This wasn't a movie.

The control—I could feel it slipping away again.

I don't know why, but for some reason, I wasn't so sure I would get it back. That gave me a chill.

I said, "He got the girl in the end and lived happily ever after."

She chuckled and said, "If your occupation were to be outed, what do you think would happen?"

I sat forward. "Excuse me?"

"You get paid to set men up. What if those men were told the truth about who you are? Do you think they'd come after you? What would happen to the women that hired you? What would happen to the comfortable lives you set up for them? Do you think you would get that happily ever after, Lisette?"

I closed my eyes a bit, drummed my fingers on the top of my desk, and said, "Who the fuck are you?"

"I told you I want you to trap my husband."

"Didn't you say he treats you like a queen?"

"My husband is an asshole!" she suddenly screamed out. "Five million dollars for every five fucking years of marriage! That's what he presented to me in a prenuptial agreement one hour before we were married. Anything less than five years and I wouldn't get shit!"

Her outburst came out of nowhere and surprised me. Made me wonder even more about who the fuck I was dealing with. I reached for my black Sidekick, found Marlene's name, and sent a text message with 9-1-1 attached. Then I asked, "Why did you sign the agreement?"

"How could I not have? The church was packed with friends and family. What was I supposed to do? Say no and then deal with the embarrassment and scrutiny of telling everyone the wedding was off? I don't think so."

"Do you love him?"

"My husband is rich. I don't have to love him."

"Then why are you so upset about the prenup? Stay in the marriage, do your time, and get your money."

"I've been living in boredom for one year. I'm not waiting four more to get a measly five million dollars. And I'm not going to waste ten years just to get more. I want money. A lot of it. And you're going to help me get that money now."

"Is that so?" I said. As I did, my black Sidekick vibrated. Marlene's response. I downloaded the message and read her reply.

She didn't know who the fuck was calling me.

She hadn't sent a client my way since our last one, three months prior.

She wanted to know who the hell I was talking to.

I did too.

I sent her another message, and then said, "What makes you so sure I'm going to help you?"

"Because unlike the movie, when people find out about what you've done, things could get ugly."

I leaned back in my chair. Interesting, I thought. This bitch really thought she had my back pinned against a wall.

My Sidekick vibrated again. I reached for it. Marlene saying she was sure she hadn't given anyone my number. She wanted me to call her ASAP. I put the Sidekick down. I was tired of this shit.

"Let me help you understand something," I said, sitting forward again. "You signed the pre-nuptial agreement, which means that as much as you think you have me backed into a corner, your ass is standing in the corner right beside me. Actually, you're standing farther back in that corner than I am, because if you out me, I'll still have something you won't have and won't ever get . . . money. You want to out me, bitch, go ahead."

And then I ended the call, grabbed my black Sidekick and called Marlene. When she answered, I said, "Meet me at Justin's in twenty minutes." I hung up before she could say anything.

Twenty minutes later, Marlene was sitting across from me.

"She didn't give you a name?"

"No."

"What about her number? Did it show up on your caller ID?"

"No. It was blocked."

Marlene shook her head and passed her hand through her hair. The same nervous habit she always had. "So what do you want to do about her?"

I thought about it for a moment, and then said, "Nothing. Fuck her."

"Are you sure? Aren't you worried about what she'll do?"

I shook my head. "No. She won't do anything, because she knows if she does, she's screwed. Fuck her," I said again.

Marlene nodded.

I nodded.

We stayed at Justin's for another hour. In that time, she told me about another client that was going to be calling me. The mysterious caller became a memory.

That changed two weeks later.

14

"We have a problem."

Diddy's restaurant again.

Lunchtime.

A table toward the back.

I'd just gotten there. Hadn't even gotten a chance to sit down yet. Marlene was seated with a half-empty martini in front of her. It was obvious by the glazed look in her eyes and the panic in her voice that she'd had more than one drink before my arrival.

I hung my Coach purse on the back of my chair and sat down. "What's the problem?"

Marlene shook her head and breathed out. "She called me." Then she swallowed down the rest of her drink, grabbed the waitress as she was walking by and ordered another. The waitress, a thin woman with breasts entirely too large for her frame, asked me if I wanted anything. I told her a glass of water and then watched her saunter off.

I looked back at Marlene. She was nervously passing her hand through her hair. "Who called you?"

"She did."

I said, "*She* could be a lot of people."

"The one who threatened to expose you. She called." Marlene cursed, said, "Where the hell is my fucking drink?" and then passed her hand through her hair again. "She threatened to tell Steve that I paid you to set him up," she said, the stress in her voice intensifying. "She said that if you don't agree to set up her husband, she's going to tell Steve that he wasn't the only husband I'd fucked over. Bitch. She called me, Lisette. She called me. How the hell did she get my number? And who the hell is she?"

Marlene looked over to the bar. Any second, she was going to get out of her chair and storm over there for her drink by her damn self. I could see it in her body language. She was tense, freaked out. This was the Marlene I remember from Houston, only magnified.

This caller; she was more resourceful than I'd given her credit for. She and I were at a stalemate. She needed me to get her money. I can't say that I really needed her too, but I preferred for her to keep her mouth shut about my business. Maybe I should have, but I hadn't thought of her going after anyone else to force my hand.

Interesting.

Marlene was tapping the index finger of her right hand repeatedly on the tabletop and staring at the bar.

I said, "Relax, Marlene."

She looked from the bar to me. Her eyes were wide, as if my words had been a slap instead. "Relax? Relax? I could lose everything I have!" she said, her voice too damned loud.

I ignored the glances in our direction and said again, "Relax."

Marlene shook her head. Passed her hand in her hair again. Began tapping her index finger once more. Seconds later, the skinny waitress with what were undoubtedly fake Ds, arrived with our drinks. Marlene grabbed hers as soon as the waitress had set it down in front of her, drank nearly half of it down, and then gave the waitress a scowl when she asked if we were ready to order. I told her that we wouldn't be eating. She nodded and—no longer worried about a tip—gave Marlene a scowl back and then walked away.

Marlene let out a laugh filled with incredulity. "You want me to relax? Lisette, you may not care about her revealing what you do—"

"What *we* do," I said, giving her a look, reminding her of her role.

She nodded. "Fine. What we do. You may not care, but I do. I took Steve to the cleaners. The child support alone that he pays is enough for me to live on. Throw in the house, the percentage of his earnings . . . if she told Steve the truth, he could literally take me to the cleaners and back again. Maybe . . . maybe you should just do it and get this bitch out of our life." She ran her hand through her hair again and then finished off the rest of her drink and looked around for the waitress again.

I shook my head. "How do you know she wasn't bluffing?"

"Because she gave details. She knew about the plan to get pregnant. She knew that he ate you out in your office. She knew about the setup at the house."

I closed my eyes a bit. "How would she have gotten that information? How did she know about what went on in my office?"

Marlene looked down at the table cloth.

"Do you know who she is?"

"No! I have no idea who she is. I've never spoken to her before."

"Then who the fuck did you talk to about what went down?" My voice was low, but Marlene could hear the ferocity behind it loud and clear.

Marlene sighed and looked at me. "Lisa. She knew."

"You said that you only told her that I had seduced Steve into sleeping with me. You said you hadn't given out any other details."

"I know. I . . . I lied."

"Obviously."

"Who else did you tell my business to?"

"No one. I swear! I was just so excited about what you'd done for me. I've known Lisa a long, long time. I didn't mean to give her details . . . they just kind of slipped out."

"From your lips to Lisa's ears. From Lisa's lips to someone else's ears."

"She wouldn't tell anyone."

"Besides her, did you let details slip to anyone else?"

Marlene dropped her chin to her chest and shook her head.

"And you don't know who this bitch is?" I pressed again.

"No."

I said, "Then it slipped from Lisa's lips too."

"I'm sorry, Lisette."

"Too late to be sorry."

"I was just . . . excited, happy."

"Your elation got you a phone call."

Marlene looked up. "Are you saying this is my fault?"

"Nothing slipped from my lips, Marlene."

"Really? What you do, never once slipped from your lips?"

"Don't challenge me, Marlene. What happened with Steve would have been known only by you and God."

Marlene opened her mouth to say something, but with nothing that she could possibly say, she closed it and began to tap her finger on the table again. After a few seconds, she said, "What should we do?"

I said, "We? I'm not doing a damn thing. You're going to figure out who this bitch is."

"How?"

"Start with Lisa and work your way through all of the clients we've had until you get a name."

"What if I don't get one?"

"If you want your life to stay the way it is now, then you better get one. Fast."

15

"Shit, Lisette . . . it . . . it's never been this . . . this . . . good. Shit."

Marlene's house.

On the couch again.

Dancing on Steve's dick.

I was windin' clockwise and then counterclockwise to a soca tune I'd listened to the other day. "Roll it," by Allison Hinds.

I loved all kinds of music. Latin, R&B, calypso, jazz, classical, hip hop. Notice I said hip hop and not crap. Crap is the rap the radio stations try to pass off as hip hop these days. It's imitation rap. I've never had time for fake bullshit, just like I've never had time for a fake-ass man. Hip hop was born in the seventies and died in the late nineties. That's what I listen to. That's real hip hop. To this day, I've never met a real-ass man.

The music I listen to on a daily basis is all
dependent on my mood at the time. The other
day, I was feeling sexy in a pink halter top and
black jeans that hugged my ass like a frightened
child clasped around his mother's leg. I was on
my way out to S.O.B's to get a drink. I was going
alone. I liked to do that. Liked to go to a club,
grab a drink, hit the floor and be noticed.

Alone.

Always alone.

I don't like to share the spotlight.

Never have.

The power of being watched turned me on.
Sometimes I'd get so turned on by the stares and
the images I knew I created in men's minds, that
I'd go home and give myself one hell of a happy
ending. Other times, I'd choose one of the admir-
ers and let him give it to me instead.

In my pink halter and black jeans, I was windin' to Allison's soca rhythm. It put me in one
hell of a mood. I went to S.O.B.'s that night and
rolled it for everyone to see. I fucked the space
around me, and then made men wish they were
fucking me when I rolled my ass against their
hard crotches on the floor.

Allison's song was in my head as I rolled it on
Steve's dick.

I had him paralyzed.

I was moving my hips side to side.

Back and forth.

Marlene had said he fucked like he invented it.

He was good. Damn good.

But I was showing him what fucking was.

I tightened the walls of my pussy around him, like a cobra squeezing the life out of its prey. Steve moaned as I felt him pulsate. He was almost there. About to explode.

I leaned back. Braced my hands around his ankles. Continued to roll it.

Then I sat up. Pressed down on him as I rolled it harder. Faster. He moaned louder. Called out my name. Reached his hands up to fondle my breasts. I pushed them away.

He said, "Shit, Lisette. Shit!"

He was at the door.

About to open it and spill inside of the condom he had on.

I constricted my walls tighter.

Rolled it harder.

Directed his dick to my spot.

Right there.

Right . . . there.

Right.

There.

And then the front door opened, and in stepped the police captain who loved it up the ass. Behind him followed the other husbands I'd set up.

I stared at them as they stared at me. Their faces were masks painted with anger, rage, and hatred.

Suddenly there was a loud growl of rage, and then something hit me in the side of my head. Hard. Near my temple. Steve's dick slid out of me as I went crashing from on top of him to the hardwood floor.

Dazed and confused, I looked up through blurred vision to see Steve standing over me with his hands balled into tight fists. His face bore the same mask as the other husbands, but he was smiling. Payback was a bitch. That's what his eyes said.

He laughed.

The other husbands laughed with him.

And then they all attacked me.

Past the swarm.

In between each punch and kick.

I saw her.

Saw her eyes.

Watching.

Reveling.

A faint whisper said, "You should have taken the money, bitch."

And then my Sidekick rang.

I opened my eyes.

I was dripping sweat. My heartbeat was thunderous. I took a breath. Gasped. My hands were shaking.

I said, "Shit."

Then I looked over at my side table beside my bed. Looked at the clock. 8:00 P.M. Didn't remember ever dozing off.

My black Sidekick was ringing. I ignored it and looked away from the clock and stared up at the ceiling for seconds, which turned into minutes.

I said, "Shit," again, and then reached for the Sidekick. I looked at the missed call. Marlene. I called her back. My hands were still shaking.

First words out of her mouth when she answered: "I know who she is."

I said, "Meet me at Justin's in half an hour."

I ended the call and stared up at the ceiling again. I valued my sleep. I hadn't had a bad dream in a long time.

This bitch was going to pay.

16

Friday night.

Diddy's restaurant.

Toward the back, for privacy again.

As always, it was packed.

People went to Justin's for two reasons. Some went for the soul food. Others went to be seen. I liked Justin's. It was suave, chic, and hip. If Diddy were a Transformer, Justin's would be what he transformed into.

I had arrived first. Ordered a Merlot to help me relax. I hated to admit it, but the dream had gotten to me. I was on edge and unnerved. I was ready to break something, someone.

I was sipping my Merlot when Marlene showed up and sat down. She ordered a martini from the waitress. When the waitress left, she gave me the name.

"Kyra Rogers."

"Kyra Rogers?" This was the first time her name escaped from my lips. Wished it would have been the last. I asked, "Do you know this bitch?"

"Never heard of her before."

Kyra Rogers.

One call to me. One call to Marlene. She'd been a presence in my world only two times, yet no one had affected me this way before.

The waitress brought Marlene her martini and left.

I said, "Did Lisa give her my number?"

Marlene shook her head. "She swears she didn't. She swears that she didn't talk about you with anyone else."

"She was the only one you gave details too, right?"

"Yes."

"Then, unless you're lying to my face, she's lying."

"I'm not lying to your face."

I stared at Marlene for a second and then said, "I know. I'd be able to tell if you were."

Marlene sipped her drink and said, "I'm sorry, Lisette. I really didn't think she'd tell anyone."

I shook my head and called Marlene a stupid bitch with my eyes.

From one pair of lips to the next.

I closed my eyes a fraction as I continued to look at Marlene. My eyes were now calling her a stupid, stupid bitch.

Marlene looked down to her glass. "I'm sorry, Lisette," she said again.

I said, "Too late for apologies."

Marlene nodded.

"So . . . what did you find out about this bitch?"

"Well, her husband's name is Myles Rogers. He's made his money by buying up real estate throughout New York City. He owns properties in Manhattan, including two hotels. He owns a lot of property in Harlem that he bought up before the resurgence. The word is when Bill Clinton moved in, it was Myles' lease that he signed."

"Kyra," I said, sipping my Merlot. "I want details about her."

Marlene raised her eyebrows. "I am giving you details about her."

"What does she do?"

"Well, other than spend her husband's money . . . nothing. She's married to a very rich African American real estate tycoon who very quietly is nipping at The Donald's heels. That's pretty much who she is. She doesn't work. She doesn't run any charitable foundations. She doesn't head any fashion companies. From what I've heard about her, she spends her time going to spas and hanging out with other wives who have nothing better to do than to hit the hot spots and hang out with rappers."

"Is she white?"

"No. She's African American."

"Black," I said. "I never liked that African American designation."

"Okay, well, she's black."

"How old is she?"

"Couldn't get a confirmation, but I'm hearing she's in her thirties."

"And Myles?"

"Fifty-three."

I sipped my Merlot.

More than women who allowed themselves to be controlled by men by taking unnecessary shit, women like Kyra pissed me off the most. They did nothing. They aspired for nothing. They were nothing. Yet they wanted everything.

I took another sip of Merlot. It was supposed to help calm me down, but the opposite was happening. My blood was starting to boil.

The bitch called and threatened me.

She called and threatened Marlene.

She didn't deserve shit, yet she wanted it all.

"Did you get a number?" I asked.

Marlene shook her head.

"That's okay. I'll get it from her husband."

"What are you planning to do?"

I looked at Marlene.

"I'm going to have a talk with Myles Rogers about two hundred thousand dollars that I could have to invest in some real estate."

17

"Your wife wants to pay me two hundred thousand dollars to trap you."

Starbucks.

Eight o'clock in the A.M.

I'd been watching Myles Rogers sip his cup of coffee for twenty minutes. He liked his coffee black. Didn't touch the Sweet-n-Low or the Splenda.

Just like Kyra said, he sat at a table alone, sipping his coffee and typing away on his Mac book. His eyes never once averted toward the counter where the twenty-something female was staring at him as though his penis were rock hard and pointing directly at her.

He sipped his coffee.

He typed on his laptop.

He ignored everything and everyone around him.

That's why he never noticed the white gentleman pretending to read a newspaper two tables over from him. Had he ever bothered to pay attention to his surroundings, he would have noticed that the man had been watching him for the past three days, just as I had been.

Myles Rogers.

He was a good looking man.

Six foot one with a runner's build. Strong, square shoulders. Attractive, intense, brown eyes with crow's feet at the corners. Slightly broad, yet distinguished nose. His lips, framed by a whisper of a goatee, were thin at the top and full at the bottom, just like Taye Diggs'. Actually, he looked a lot like him. But Taye was a sexy, bald specimen, whereas Myles had gray curls. Even with the gray, I wouldn't have put him a day over forty.

Myles. Married to that bitch.

I Googled them on the Internet after my meeting with Marlene. I wanted to put faces with the names.

Myles—an attractive fifty-two-year-old Taye Diggs look-a-like.

Kyra.

I wanted her to be as ugly as her personality. I wanted her to be a black Cruela DeVille. But my wishes weren't satisfied. She looked like the queen bee, Lil' Kim before she decided she'd look better with plastic parts.

Pretty eyes.

Pretty nose.

Pretty smile.

Pretty teeth.

Just all around pretty.

I might have even called her sexy. But I had no love for her, so pretty was as far as I'd take it.

She looked like someone I knew from the neighborhood I'd grown up in. Or maybe someone I knew looked like her. Whatever it was, there was just something about her that was very around the way. Made me wonder what it was about her that guided her toward him.

I took a sip of the espresso I'd ordered and watched Myles tap dance his fingers on his laptop. Then I switched to the man Kyra had hired.

Mid to late forties.

Scraggly beard.

Bags under his eyes.

Looked like he'd rather be somewhere else, and would have been if it weren't for the money he was being paid.

I sipped my espresso in the cheap paper cup until the heat went away. Then I approached scraggly beard.

"I'll double whatever she's paying you."

He looked up at me, confusion in his eyes. "Huh?"

"You've been watching him tap away on his laptop for twenty minutes. You'll do that for another twenty and then you'll follow him to his office. You'll take a break for a few hours and then, if he steps out for lunch, you'll follow him there and back. You'll take a break again for another few hours, and then you'll follow him back to Starbucks and then home. The routine was the same yesterday. It won't change today. It'll be the same tomorrow and the day after that. If I were you, I'd take me up on my offer and then go and find something better to do."

Scraggly beard's forehead knotted up. He wanted to know if I was kidding. Or maybe even testing him.

I said, "The bitch who hired you doesn't have sense enough to test you this way."

He looked at me, then looked over in Myles' direction, and back to me. He said, "Ten thousand."

I reached into my purse and pulled out my checkbook.

I filled out a blank check and handed it to him. I said, "Good-bye."

He looked from me to Myles again, and then shrugged, snatched the check from my hand, gathered up the newspaper, and left. Two minutes after that, I was sitting down at Myles' table, telling him that his wife wanted to pay me to trap him.

He looked up from his laptop. "Excuse me?"

"Your wife offered me two hundred thousand dollars to seduce you. She wants your money, and she doesn't want to wait five years to get any of it."

Myles looked at me with his mouth partly open. "Are you kidding me?"

"No."

He looked around the café.

I said, "No hidden cameras."

He put his focus back on me. "You're serious?"

"I've never liked games."

"Two hundred thousand?"

"I'm sure I could get her to pay more."

He watched me.

He saw the dead seriousness in my eyes.

He took a breath.

He let it out.

He closed his laptop.

18

"Who are you?"

"My name doesn't matter. What does matter is that your wife threatened me. She also threatened the lives of a few women that I do business with."

Myles shook his head. "I . . . I don't understand."

"Why did you marry her?"

"Excuse me?"

"You had two failed marriages. That was no reason to settle for a gold-digging bitch."

"How did you know about my marriages?"

"Your wife told me."

Myles' forehead knotted up in frustration.

I said, "She told me a lot, Myles."

"I . . . I don't believe this," he said, his voice laced with the same disbelief present in his eyes.

"She's tried to set you up before."

His eyes widened.

I continued. "High-priced hookers. Men. Nothing worked, though. You never gave in to temptation. Why?"

"I . . . I love my wife. I . . ." He paused, clamped his hand down around the back of his neck and squeezed. "I can't believe this," he said again. "I don't believe it. I don't believe you."

Strong conviction in the tone of his voice.

Nothing but doubt, shock and anxiety in his eyes.

I said, "You come to Starbucks every morning for your coffee. You sit here and type away on your laptop for forty minutes. You leave here and go to work. Sometimes you take lunch. Most of the time you don't. After work, you come back here for your wind-down fix and then you go home, give your wife a peck on her cheek, and then disappear to your study to do more work."

Myles looked at me. He was stunned. He didn't understand how or why this twilight zone moment was happening.

"How . . ."

"Your wife's been having you followed, hoping to catch you doing something you shouldn't be doing. She's tried and failed. I'm good, Myles. Nothing like those high-priced hoes she hired. Had I said yes to her, in another month, you would have been on your way to being severely hurt, financially."

Myles squeezed the back of his neck again. His brain was struggling to absorb my words. His heart couldn't contemplate the level of betrayal I'd just presented. It just didn't make sense to him.

"Are you pussy-whipped, Myles?"

His mouth dropped a notch. "Excuse me?" "Is her pussy magical? Does she do things that make your toes curl?"

Myles looked around the café to see who else heard my questions. Luckily for him, no one had been paying attention.

Still, he leaned closer to me and dropped the volume in his voice. "That's none of your fucking business."

I stared at him. His language surprised me. Up until that point, I didn't think he had it in him. I crossed my legs. I was wearing a sleeveless, lavender blouse with a slouch collar that clung to my frame. I had on a black skirt with a slit at the side, which stopped just above the knee. My leg was peeking through the slit, revealing a lot of thigh.

Myles tried not to, but he looked.

High-priced hoes could be attractive, but they didn't have it like I did. They did what they did to survive. I did what I did because I could. High-priced hookers thought they understood what being confident was all about, but the truth of the matter was, they didn't understand shit. That's why they could never get a man like Myles to fold and do as men did.

Myles admired my leg for only a few seconds, but a few seconds was all that was needed.

Fuck a ho.

I was the real deal.

I gave Myles a subtle smile and said, "I already know all of your fucking business."

He wanted to say something. He opened his mouth to do just that. Then he closed it and squeezed his neck again. He couldn't say anything.

"Did you really think a prenup would protect you?"

Myles sighed.

His shoulders sagged.

Reality was sinking in.

"I don't understand. Kyra ... she ... she wouldn't do this to me. I mean, she loves me."

"Are you asking or telling?"

Myles squeezed his neck again and then moved from there to his temples. "What the fuck?" he said, dragging his hand down over his face. "What the fuck?"

I said, "Kyra's a bitch. She never loved you."

Myles blinked rapidly several times and then his shoulders sagged a little more.

My statement was blunt and raw. Had it been a knife, he would have bled to death.

"I've never met her face to face, but it only took one conversation to know she's a gold digger, and my saying that has nothing to do with her wanting to hire me. Her personality comes through in the tone of her voice . . . the way she says her words. You were played by an ignorant bitch."

Myles shook his head and stared out the window of the café. "I can't believe this," he said, with genuine hurt in his voice. "This just doesn't seem real to me."

"Believe it," I said. "Because this is very real."

He sighed again and looked back at me. "She never . . . her qualities . . . she's so genuine."

"But yet you made her sign a prenup an hour before you married her."

"I was just . . ." He paused and clenched his jaws. "I mean, I'd had it drawn up as a precaution, but I'd decided not to give it to her. But people kept pushing me. Saying after the drama with my first two wives, that I couldn't be caught out there again. That I had to give it to her."

I closed my eyes a bit. "So the only reason you gave it to her was because of other people?"

Myles nodded. "I just didn't think I needed it. Not with her."

"You're a fool," I said. "Now I wish I wouldn't have said anything."

"Why did you? Are you looking for more of a pay off from me?"

"I don't want shit from you."

He shook his head. "Damn. I thought it was real. I thought she was the one."

"You thought wrong."

Myles clenched his jaws again. "Bitch," he said. "Fucking bitch. I can't believe she was trying to set me up."

"Like I said . . . you're a fool."

Myles looked at me. He didn't like the truth one bit.

"You're not looking for money?"

"Had I been, I would have had two hundred thousand dollars already."

Myles straightened his back and stuck his chest out a little. "Aren't you being a little overconfident?"

As he said that, his eyes roamed from my eyes to my breasts, and then down to my legs again.

I said, "Don't play yourself, Myles."

He looked back up at me with concession in his eyes. "I guess I'm indebted to you."

"I told you, I don't want anything."

"My wife was going to pay you to seduce me. You don't have to be here sitting in front of me right now. I owe you something."

I stared at him for a few seconds and then grabbed my purse. My mission had been accomplished. He would go home and Kyra's world would be fucked. I stood up to leave. "Goodbye, Myles."

Before I could walk away, he grabbed me by my wrist. I looked at his fingers clamped around me, and then at him. He was staring at me intensely.

He said, "My wife was going to pay you two hundred thousand dollars of my money to seduce me."

I said, "Yes. She was."

He said, "She's going to pay."

I said, "Good."

"She's not going to get shit."

"Good."

"I'm pissed."

"You should be."

"I don't condone violence on women, but if she were here, I'd slap the shit out of her."

"I'd join you."

"Bitch. I thought she was different."

"Why are you still holding on to my wrist?"

"Two hundred thousand," he said, his index finger moving against my skin softly.

"Two hundred thousand," I repeated.

He looked from side to side for eavesdroppers and then said, "I'll give you three hundred thousand."

He continued to caress the inside of my wrist with his finger, as he stared at me with eyes filled with anger, hurt, and lust. Vengeful eyes. Eyes that said, *My wife was going to try to screw me out of millions. Now I'm going to be the one to do the screwing.*

"Three hundred thousand for what?"

"To fuck me."

"She hired high-priced hookers. I'm not one."

"I'm not implying that you are."

"You want to pay me three hundred thousand to fuck you."

He shook his head. "No."

"No?"

"No. I want to pay you three hundred thousand dollars to let *me* fuck *you*."

"So you're not buying my company?"

"No. I'm paying you for mine."

"What if I don't want the company?"

He stood up. I'm five foot five. He was at least seven inches taller. Made me wonder about how many other inches he had.

His hand still around my wrist, he said, "You just told me that my wife wanted to pay you to set me up. I'm pissed right now. I want to fuck."

I licked my lips. "Angry sex is good sex."

"It would be great sex."

I looked at him.

He looked at me.

We stood staring for seconds.

His hand was still vice-gripped around my wrist.

He needed the release.

He needed to vent.

He had no intention of letting me go.

Three hundred thousand to be fucked.

Angrily.

Without feeling.

Without compassion.

Just sex.

Fucking.

I said, "Grab your laptop."

19

Angry sex is the most intense sex to have. It's hard. It's rough. It's uncaring. It's uninhibited. It's also completely self-gratifying.

I was on my knees. My hands were braced against the headboard of the bed. Myles was behind me, penetrating my pussy hard, deep. Each thrust was for his pleasure and pain. How it felt to me meant nothing.

We spoke no words.

Had been silent since we'd stepped into the suite he paid for.

We were there to fuck.

Small talk had happened at Starbucks.

Grunts. Moans. *Oohs*. *Aahs*.

This was all the conversation we needed.

I bit down on my bottom lip and backed my ass up as he came forward.

Myles groaned.

Speaking to him with my body only, I told him, *Fuck me harder, deeper.* Said, *Show me what you got.* Asked, *How pissed are you? How much do you hate that bitch?*

With his thrusts, he said, *I fucking hate her.*

I backed up, squeezed my walls around him, said, *Show me. Fuck me. Fuck the shit out of me.*

He came forward.

I backed up.

Is that all you have?

No, I have more. Much more.

Then bring it.

I will.

Good.

Is that better?

Getting.

Now?

Mmm. Close.

Like this?

Oooh.

Hard enough?

Yes.

Is it hurting enough?

Yesss!

Good. Take it. Take it.

I backed up harder, making his penetration even more forceful.

Give it to me, Myles.

He grunted.

Moved faster.

Harder.

I gnawed on my bottom lip a little harder. It hurt. Hurt so good. He was pissed. So, so pissed.

I moaned.

I moaned.

I moaned.

I got chills.

And then from my G-spot, from my clit, from the walls of my pussy, I came. Came damn hard.

Myles grunted as my levees broke. Grunted, moaned, made sounds that were borderline demonic.

"Can't . . . can't hold it. About . . . to . . . about to . . . Shit . . . shit . . . shit!"

And then he came.

Fierce.

Powerful.

Almost sent me into the headboard as he thrust forward.

He leaned forward against me and jerked a few times as he released the rest of his jism into the condom he had on. He was breathing heavily. His heart was beating even heavier. He jerked several more times until the sensitivity died down. Then he pulled out of me and rolled over onto his back.

I turned and sat with my back against the headboard. My legs were stretched out in front of me. I didn't cover up. I usually never let a man run the show, but Myles wanted to pay me three hundred thousand dollars to fuck me. I wanted to see if he could put his money where his mouth was.

I let out a slow breath. I didn't smoke, but if I did, I'd be taking long drags on a cigarette right then and there. But I'd tried smoking once in fifth grade, hated the taste, and never tried again.

He was good. Shit . . . better than good. One of the best I'd ever been with. I was impressed. I looked down at him. "Are you still pissed?"

He looked up at me. "Very. Going to be a while before I'm not."

"It's obvious that you settled with her. Why?" I was curious.

He propped himself up on his elbows. His dick, still in the condom, was limp and lay on his thigh. I hadn't had an opportunity to see how well equipped he was before, because seconds after we stepped into the suite, he took me to the bed, turned me around, stripped me, removed his own clothing, and then bent me over. Fully erect with the blood pumping, it had been a force. It still held its own in its current state.

I looked at him.

He'd been watching me stare.

With his eyes, he said there was more to be had.

With mine, I said, *I may have to take you up on that.*

He cleared his throat and then sighed. "She wasn't anything like my other two wives. My first two were . . . refined. More sophisticated. But Kyra . . . there was just an appeal about her. She wasn't afraid to speak her mind. She just seemed so much more genuine. So much more real. When she said something, she meant it. When she told me that she loved me, I believed it because I just could not see her saying something and not meaning it.

"My first two wives, I married them because they were essentially the type of black women I was supposed to marry. Good background. Good, affluent families."

"Good pedigree," I said.

He nodded. "I guess you could say that."

"But they turned out to be bitches."

"To say the least."

"They were both younger, weren't they?"

"Yes."

"You have a thing for young, gold-digging pussy."

He looked at me and then frowned. "Apparently."

"You're a fool," I said, shaking my head. "You got burned twice, yet people had to push you into giving Kyra the prenup."

"Like I said, I thought she was different."

I said, "She was. She turned out to be the super bitch."

Myles chuckled. "I guess so."

I shook my head again. "You're lucky I dislike her so damn much, because you deserve to get burned again."

Myles shrugged. His ego was taking a beating. "Here's to her being a super bitch."

"Here's to you being another woman's fool."

"That's not going to happen again."

"Is that a statement or a question?"

"A vow. I've been at bat three times and I struck out. I'm done with marriage and trying to find that one person. I've had enough headaches to last a lifetime." Myles sighed and lay back on the bed.

"Marriage is overrated," I said. "A waste of time."

"Have you ever been?"

"No."

"Ever wanted to be?"

"No."

"Haven't you ever had a desire to share your life with someone?"

"I don't like to share."

"Have you ever been in love?"

"Once."

"And what happened?"

"Love turned to hate."

"Not all men are bad, you know."

"Enough of them are."

"I don't consider myself one."

"No. You're just a fool."

"Not anymore."

"That remains to be seen."

Myles sighed and stared up at the ceiling. After a few seconds, he said, "You and I . . . the sex was good. Damn good."

I said. "Angry sex."

He said, "Best kind." He was silent for another few seconds and then said, "I cooled down for a moment, but talking about her has me pissed off again."

He looked over at me.

I looked at him.

Minutes later, we were in the shower fucking.

My legs wrapped around his waist.

My nails digging into the flesh of his back.

His palms at my sides, laying flat against the tiles.

Just like on the bed, I let myself go, and swallowed him deep. Took every inch he had to offer and opened myself up to take even more. My pussy rained down like the water that was beating on us like applause.

I sucked on his ear lobe as he pushed himself up inside of me. I nibbled on it when he pulled out and demanded that he slam back up into me.

With each thrust, I let go.

Let go and let Myles.

Fuck me.

Fuck me.

Fuck . . . me.

Myles made demonic noises again and then told me how good my pussy was. How tight it was. "Never . . . never had pussy like this," he said. "Shit . . . never."

I said, "You never will again."

He slammed up into me and said, "I know."

I arched my back, giving him more to work with.

Myles grabbed me by my waist and thrust his dick so hard up into me I gasped.

Gasped and then moaned.

Said, "Do it again."

And again.

And again.

And again.

And then harder and more powerful than before, I came.

Minutes later, it was Myles' turn to release every drop he had.

Completely spent, we remained in the shower, connected as one as the water cascaded down over us. We had sex one more time after that before he left to go and turn Kyra's world upside down.

20

Something wasn't right. I could feel it.

I was standing in front of my door. I'd just come home after another night of kick boxing at the gym. I was tired. I had turned up the intensity in class. Had everyone kicking, punching, blocking until they couldn't anymore. No one had come expecting to be worked so hard. To be honest, I never intended on pushing them the way I had. But Myles and the sex we'd had just a week before had been on my mind, and that was frustrating the hell out of me.

He'd worked it. Worked it so good that as much as I wanted to, I couldn't stop thinking about it. The way he'd pounded me. The way he controlled me.

Initially, I'd given up the control to see if he could back up the talking. Eventually, control became something that I couldn't get back. I'd turned up the intensity in class because I wanted to kick and punch away the thought of wanting Myles to dominate my pussy again. But it didn't work. The more I fought against the desire, the more I wanted to Myles up inside of me again.

Luckily for the class, my time slot had only been for an hour and a half, because the way I felt, I could have kicked and punched for a hell of a lot longer.

Completely fatigued, my plan was to go home, take a hot shower, have a glass of wine, and then go to sleep with Pink Martini playing in the background. But standing in front of my door, the feeling causing bumps to rise from my skin told me that relaxing night I'd planned wasn't going to happen.

I put my hand on the doorknob. The feeling was strong. Something wasn't right at all. I felt it like hot breath on the back of my neck. I felt it like I was still feeling Myles inside of me. It was intense. It was dangerous.

I tested the knob by trying to turn it. It failed the test when it did turn. I let my Nike bag fall from my shoulder, balled my hands into fists, shifted my feet into a fighting stance for proper balance, took a deep breath, and then pushed my door open.

When it opened completely, my breath escaped from my lungs as I stared at complete destruction. My flat-screen plasma television was lying face down on the ground, destroyed. My Italian leather sofa and chaise had been ripped to shreds. My expensive oriental porcelain statues had been shattered. My coffee table and side tables had been broken beyond repair. My vertical blinds had been ripped down, along with various paintings, which had all been defaced as well.

I stepped inside and stared at the violation that had taken place. My tower of CDs that I had for display since everything was on my iPod, lay scattered and broken. My shelf system and books I had on shelves . . . everything. I looked toward the bedroom. Saw my door, which I never left open, completely ajar. I unclenched my hands. Without doing a walk-through, I knew I was alone.

My Sidekick rang suddenly. I looked at the caller ID. Marlene. I answered.

"L . . . Lisette."

She was crying.

"Marlene. What's wrong?"

She cried hard tears for a few seconds before speaking. "Kyra . . . she . . . she told Steve."

I walked to my bedroom to see the damage done there. "Told Steve what, Marlene?"

"She told him everything. He knows that I paid you to set him up. He just called me. He says he's taking me to court. He says he's going to take Ben away from me." She broke down again.

I frowned and shook my head as I stared at the complete disheveling that had taken place in my room. I said, "Calm down, Marlene."

"Calm down? Did you just hear what I said? Steve knows!"

I picked up a pair of Mavi jeans that I loved. The front and back had been cut up. I shook my head and tossed them to the ground. Kept looking around. Said, "What does he know, Marlene? What exactly can he prove?"

"She . . . she told him everything, Lisette. She even told him about being in your office."

I thought about that episode and smiled. Steve and his tongue had worked it out. I bent down and picked up a sequinned blouse I'd designed for a famous pop singer several months ago. The blouse, along with the rest of the line, was supposed to have been the hottest line for the summer. Unfortunately, the twenty-something phenomenon lost whatever grasp she'd had on the drugs and alcohol she was consuming on a daily basis, and was now in and out of rehab. As a result, the line was put on hold. The blouse had been the only one made. I tossed it to the bed and looked around at all of my other things that had been ruined.

"Marlene . . . haven't you learned anything by now?"

"But—"

"But nothing, Marlene. What's Steve going to do? Tell the judge that I forced him to eat my pussy and fuck me on his couch while he thought you were away on a business trip? Marlene, no matter what the hell he knows, the fact is he cheated on you and you caught him in the act, with a witness at your side. A judge won't do shit for him, so relax."

I bent down and picked up a Manolo pump—the left shoe—and sighed. Its soft brown leather had been stabbed over and over and cut. The more I walked around and looked at the destruction of my things, the angrier I found myself becoming. Truthfully, it wasn't the fact that my shit had been destroyed that was pissing me off because I was insured and could buy the things back. What was really stoking the fire inside of me was the fact that the cowardly bitch, Kyra, had dared to invade my space. There wasn't any indication that it was her who had broken in, but I knew it was her.

Bitch.

Marlene said, "Steve's going to tell people that I set him up. I just know it. My family, my friends . . . they're all going to look at me differently."

"Fuck your family and fuck your friends, Marlene. Shit."

"I just—"

"Marlene, I have to go. I have bigger things to deal with."

"But what about the other clients?"

"What about them?"

"She's probably going to tell their husbands too."

In my bathroom, the glass had been shattered, my makeup completely ruined, everything in the medicine cabinet and underneath the sink had been emptied, opened and spilled. Tiles in my shower were cracked. My glass doors broken.

Bitch, I thought again. *Fucking pathetic bitch*.

I said, "Get your shit together, Marlene, and then call them and make sure they get their shit together too."

I hung up the phone without another word. I was standing back within the ruins of my living room.

Kyra.

I said her name over and over in my head.

She'd done what no one had been able to do in a long time: she'd gotten under my skin.

I took a breath. Clenched my jaws. Balled my hands into fists again.

Bitch.

I exhaled slowly, trying to center myself. I needed to center myself. Needed to follow the advice I'd given Marlene. I needed to get my shit together because I could feel myself losing it, and that was something I hadn't done in a long, long time.

I took another deep breath and let it out. As I did, my silver Sidekick rang. Marlene had just called me on my black one. Silver was for business. I hadn't taken on any new clients recently. There was only one person that could have been calling me.

I hit the TALK button, but didn't say anything.

Kyra said, "How do you like the new look of your home, bitch?"

I clenched my jaws and balled my hand into a tight fist again. Her voice and the scene around me: I was supposed to have been trying to keep my composure, but the combination was making it damn hard. I said, "I assume Myles kicked you out on your ass?"

Kyra laughed. "You should have taken the fucking money."

I thought about the sex and the three hundred thousand Myles had given me and said, "Myles fucked me and gave me three hundred thousand dollars. I did take your money, bitch. And more."

"You fucking trick! You have no idea what you've brought on yourself. Your apartment was just for starters."

"You didn't accomplish shit by coming here, Kyra, because I can buy back everything you've destroyed. What the fuck can you buy back now?"

Kyra laughed again.

Something about it made bumps rise from my skin.

"No idea, you whore. You have no idea what you're in for."

"Let me give you some good advice, Kyra. Don't fuck with me anymore. I'm not the one you want to fuck with. Believe me."

"No, let *me* give *you* some advice," she said, her tone ominous. "Watch your back."

"Talk doesn't mean shit to me, Kyra."

Kyra chuckled. "You just don't know, bitch. I'll be doing a whole lot more than talking."

"Threats don't scare me."

"I'm not threatening you, ho! I'm promising that you're going to regret ever going to Myles."

"You know where I live, Kyra. Bring it."

"Trust me, Lisette, you will regret those words."

"We'll see."

I ended the call and threw the Sidekick across the room. My heart was pounding. Beads of sweat had formed on my forehead. My hands were shaking. I took a breath and held it in an attempt to calm down again. Closed my eyes and counted backwards from one hundred. Told myself to relax. Calm down. Pleaded with myself to not lose it any more than I already had. Not again.

Years ago with my ex, I'd lost it. Lost it bad. The day I'd gotten medieval on him is one I'd never forget. That was the day Lisette had truly been born.

I exhaled and as I did, the memories of that moment came flooding back in my mind.

His living room.

Lights dimmed low.

Music playing from the CD player. Luther. "Always and Forever."

It was supposed to have been a romantic evening. He'd been promoted at work. He wanted to celebrate.

We were dancing, kissing. As we did, his hands slid beneath the skirt I had on, and his fingers made their way up. But it was that time of the month for me, so before he could go too far, I stopped him. Told him it was the first of my seven days. Said he couldn't have me, but I'd make sure he had a happy ending.

One thing about my ex: after the first six months of bliss, he became an ass. When he drank, he became worse. Before the wine we'd shared, he'd damn near had a bottle of Henny by himself. He was drunk, horny, and not interested in what time of the month it was.

He grabbed me. Told me he didn't give a shit about a happy ending. He wanted his pussy. I pushed him away from me. Told him again that we couldn't have intercourse. He backhanded me across the mouth. I don't know why, but I'd endured the abuse before.

But that night . . .

I don't know what was particularly different about it, but that night, instead of taking it, I raised my head, then my hand, which I'd balled up, and hit him back. Hard.

The shock in his eyes, I'd never forget. He couldn't believe that I'd hit him. He called me a fucking bitch, and this time, punched me. I almost went down, and maybe on a different day I would have, but that night, instead of falling, I caught my balance, let out a growl from somewhere deep within me, and lunged toward him.

I punched.

I kicked.

I kneed.

I spat.

I bit.

He was stronger, taller, and outweighed me by at least fifty pounds, but that night, his strength and size meant nothing. He couldn't contain me. He couldn't handle the rage I'd been harboring deep inside for so long. Years of rage. Rage against my father for fucking me with his eyes. Rage against my mother for abandoning me to be violated. He couldn't handle it.

And neither could I.

That's when the Lisette that I am now came to be. My former self would never have bitten flesh from his hand. She would never have dug her fingers into his eye sockets. Most certainly, she would never have grabbed the marble paperweight in the shape of a Black Power fist and used that to bash him in his head over and over and over again. The former Lisette would have been lying on her back, letting her ex swim in her bloody sea.

That night . . .

My ex died.

I haven't been that person since.

I should have gone to jail. Should be there now. But the way my lawyer presented it, I was a battered woman who'd been defending herself. The jury, which consisted of six women, sided with me and I was found not guilty.

I took slow, deep breaths.

I had to get it together.

For her sake, Kyra needed to be more mouth than action.

21

"Why did you set me up?" I was working late, going over a few preliminary designs for another pop princess the company had signed as a client.

Julianna.

She was supposed to be the new Madonna, only with a better voice and a more brazen persona than the Material Girl ever had.

I'd seen a few of her videos. Caught a couple of performances on TV. She had a stronger voice. But the passion and delivery weren't there. As for her persona: Madonna knew how to slap you in the face with what she had, but she also knew how to make you admire what she had been doing whether you wanted to or not. She was sexy and worked her entire package so well, she became a legend.

Julianna had sex appeal, but she didn't know how to work it at all. Her videos, her performances . . . the way she presented herself to the fans and the media—everything about her was in your face. Part of the reason for that had to do with the fact that she was only eighteen years old. Let's face it, she wasn't yet a woman. The other part of the reason for her over-the-top persona had to do with the pressure within the industry. These days, if you wanted to make it to the top of the charts, you pretty much had to strip and fuck in the videos. Julianna had potential, but unless she grew balls and stopped letting everyone else run her show, she was going to end up fading as quickly as Brittney Spears' good-girl reputation.

I put down the red pen I'd been making notes with and looked up. Steve was standing in the doorway. Despite having put on a couple of pounds, he was still an appealing white man. I couldn't help it: my mind drifted back to the last office visit he'd made.

I said, "I didn't set you up, Steve. You did that all by yourself."

Steve's eyes closed a fraction. He stepped inside and closed the door behind him. "You fucking bitch," he said, his voice laced with venom. "You set me up." He took a step toward my desk. I thought about the dream I'd had where the tables had been turned and I'd been the one being set up. "What the fuck did I ever do to you?"

My eyes on his, I said, "Nothing."

Steve took another step forward. "Then why? Why did you have to fuck up my life?"

I stared at him as he took heavy breaths. He wanted to reach across my desk and wrap his fingers around my throat. He wanted to squeeze until there was no life left. I could see it in his eyes. I could see it in his body language. I thought of the dream again. He'd had balls in the dream, but in real life it was a different story.

I said, "I didn't fuck up your life, Steve. You did that yourself when you decided that you had to have my pussy."

Steve slammed his palms on my desktop. "You conniving whore! You knew what you were doing to me! You knew I couldn't resist you!"

I rolled my chair back and stood up. "Couldn't you?" I walked around the desk slowly. Behind the anger, behind the rage, there'd been something else in Steve's eyes. Something that, no matter how bitter he was, would never go away.

Lust.

I stood in front of him and stared up at him. There was so much anger, yet still so much desire radiating from him. "Why couldn't you resist me, Steve?"

He clenched his jaws and tried not to peruse my body. He didn't want to be turned on. Didn't want to think about me riding him again. But I could tell that's exactly what he was doing. Imagining me on top. On the couch again. Undisturbed. Fucking hard. Fucking deep.

I licked my lips. Put my hand over his hard crotch. "Why?" I asked again.

Steve swallowed saliva and cleared his throat. "You're . . . you're . . ."

I licked my lips again. "I'm?"

Steve's dick jumped. I squeezed it. Made it jump and grow more. "What am I, Steve?"

He swallowed saliva again. Said, "You're . . . a bitch."

My hand still squeezing him, I stepped toward him and put my lips right beside his earlobe. "You don't mean that," I whispered as I massaged.

He nodded slowly. "I do. I mean . . . it. You're a . . . a . . . a fucking bitch."

I licked the bottom of his earlobe. "You know what, Steve? I'd rather be a fucking bitch than a fucking pussy like you. Now, get the fuck out of my office."

I let go of his crotch and walked back to my chair.

Steve clenched his jaws again and flared his thin nostrils. "You fucking bitch. I'm not going to let you get away with this."

"Unless you want your ass to be escorted out by two very hefty black men, I suggest you do what I said and get the fuck out. Now." I kept my eyes on him and reached for the phone as he glared back at me with evil intent in his eyes.

He shook his head. He wanted to say to hell with the security guards and dive across the desk to get at me. It was obvious in his eyes and in the scowl he gave me.

He shook his head again, thought about it for another second, and then backpedaled toward the door. He hated me, but he wasn't that stupid.

"This isn't over, Lisette. You can't just fuck with people's lives and get away with it. You're not as untouchable as you think you are."

"Three seconds, Steve." I pressed one of the buttons on the key pad. "And don't think about coming back."

Steve gave me another menacing stare. It actually gave me the chills. I pressed another number.

"You're going to fucking pay, bitch."

"You mean the way you did?"

Steve clenched his jaws. His body language said he was ready to charge.

I pressed another button and said, "One more number and security will be here in less than a minute."

Steve bared his teeth, called me a bitch again, and then finally turned, opened the door and walked out.

I stood still behind my desk for several seconds with my finger inches above the last number. Again, the dream ran through my mind. I'd handled Steve with a lot of bravado, but the truth of the matter was, I had been nervous.

When I was sure that he wasn't coming back, I put the phone back down in the cradle and sat down. I grabbed my pen again to get back to looking at the preliminary designs for Julianna's line. That's when I noticed my hands were shaking.

I put the pen down, laid my palms flat on my desk top.

I breathed.

Tried to relax.

Tried not to think about the dream or that bitch again.

Tried not to think about the look in Steve's eyes.

Tried to get centered.

A few minutes later, I gathered the designs, grabbed my purse and my car keys.

Breathing and relaxing hadn't done shit for me.

I needed the gym. I needed to work out my anxiety.

I left and went to the gym and worked on my arms and back. I ran the treadmill for an hour and a half. Then I moved to the StairMaster for another hour. Climbed until the burning in my legs and hips demanded that I stop. When my body and mind both had enough, I called it a day and headed home. My plan was to wash off the sweat in my new shower I'd had installed, sit on my new leather sofa, have a glass of wine, and finish going over the preliminary designs.

That never happened.

22

Thunder exploding. Lightning crackling, brightening the black sky for seconds at a time.

Raindrops, falling fast, heavy and hard.

I watched all of this as I lay on the ground, while the rain beat down on me. Barely conscious, I bled from the back of my head, my nose, and my mouth. I took a slow breath. It was a painful one. Felt like my insides were on fire. I coughed and the temperature of the fire increased.

Tears snaked from my eyes and mixed with the rain water pooling on the concrete around me. I didn't want to, but I had no choice—I took another breath. Inhaling and exhaling hurt so badly, I swore I wasn't going to take another. I was just going to lay still, let my swelling right eye close completely, let whatever air in my body I had left sigh away, and then die. As lightning cracked, as thunder boomed, that's what I decided to do. But . . .

As badly as my upper body was hurting.

As badly as my lower body . . . my lower body . . . my . . . lower . . . body . . .

As badly as I wanted to give in to the pain I was enduring.

As badly as I wanted to give up.

I just couldn't, because despite the pain and agony, two facts remained. One—I was still breathing, and two—because I was, that meant that the bitch hadn't succeeded.

I tried to move, but a sharp pain where my ribs were made it too difficult. I waited for a few seconds, and then after another pain-filled breath, I tried to ignore the pain and will myself to move. Unfortunately, at that moment, my will just wasn't strong enough, and so I just lay still beneath the storm.

Unmoving.

Breathing.

Hurting.

Thinking.

Remembering . . .

Leaving the gym. Hurrying across the virtually empty parking lot through the downpour to my car, which I'd always made a habit of parking in the farthest lane to give my legs one extra workout. Had I known a monsoon was coming, I would have parked much closer.

I was hurrying, but I was hurrying slowly. I was tired. Physically drained from the workout I'd put my body through. Mentally drained from the thoughts about Kyra and her threats, to Steve and his.

On the StairMaster I said to hell with Julianna and the designs. I just wanted to get home, take a hot shower, listen to the new Pink Martini CD I'd bought, stretch out on my couch in my satin robe with nothing on underneath, have a glass of Brunello Di Montalcino, and relax. That's where my focus was. Not on the rain. Not on thunder and lightning. Not on the person coming up behind me as I opened my car door.

Simultaneously, thunder exploded, lightning flashed, and something hit me hard in the back of my head. I fell forward against my car. As I did, my assailant hit me in my ribs, then grabbed me by my shoulders, pulled me back, and then slammed me into my car repeatedly.

I was dazed and on the verge of passing out from the blow to my head, but somehow my survival instincts kicked in, and when the attacker went to slam me forward again, I snapped my head back, ramming it into their shoulder just enough forcing them to let me go. My legs were unsteady, but I managed to turn around and face my attacker.

Wide, thick shoulders. At least six foot tall. Dressed in all black, with a black ski mask and black gloves on. Without question, my attacker was male.

I got into my fighting stance, balled my fists and quickly swung out at him, connecting with a left cross in his face before he could attack me again. I followed that up with a hard kick to the side of his left knee. In the movies, the assailant usually went down after that. Real life was different.

Still on his feet, he swung out with a right of his own, hitting me in my mouth and splitting my lip instantly. Next he caught me in my nose with a left, and then another right in my eye. Before I could register how badly the punches had hurt, he lunged forward and rammed his shoulder into my midsection, sending me staggering backward. I tried to keep my balance, but I lost my footing on the flooded ground and fell backward, where the back of my head took another blow as it bounced off of the concrete.

There was no more fight after that.

As my head throbbed and everything around me faded in and out, my attacker knelt beside me. I turned my head slightly, trying to get a look at his eyes. I wanted to see if I knew him. Unfortunately, the rain drops and the flashing spots made it impossible for me to focus.

The attacker leaned forward and brought his mouth beside my ear. For a long couple of seconds, he didn't speak. He just breathed. Maybe even laughed a little. But then my ears were ringing, so I couldn't be sure.

Finally, he said in a whisper, "Kyra sends her regards."

Kyra.

Cowardly bitch couldn't even handle her own shit.

I was fading. In a few minutes, unconsciousness was going to claim me. After that . . .

I'd never thought about dying before, but at that moment I did. Was it going to be quick? Was I going to be made to suffer? When death finally claimed me, which direction was I going to go? Up? Down? These questions and more ran through my mind in a matter of seconds.

What was the meaning of life?

Of death?

What was the meaning of my life?

What was my purpose?

I was a home wrecker. Was that my reason for being?

Was that going to get me past the pearly gates, or was that going to get me a seat in eternal damnation?

I'd never been a religious person. My mother tried to force feed the Bible to me, but I took after my father and preferred devil horns and mischief to the halo and innocence. Every now and then God and I chatted, but for the most part, we left each other alone. Or at least I left Him alone. Was that why this was happening to me now? Was this my punishment?

I was about to die.

Or so I thought.

My attacker chuckled again, or at least I thought he did, and then he grabbed the waistband of my sweats and began to pull them down.

I was dizzy.

I was nauseated.

I was weak.

I was about to pass out.

I was about to be raped.

It was hard, but I found the will and strength to move my arms and legs to try to fight him off of me, despite his weight.

He slapped me.

Kneed me in my side and continued to yank my sweats and thong down below my ass.

I continued to fight.

My arms, flailing.

Hitting him.

Pushing him.

My legs, still trying to kick, knee—anything.

He slapped me again.

Then punched me.

Hard. Two . . . three . . . four times.

The world spun.

The black became blacker.

I tried to fight again.

He punched and kneed me again.

The speed of everything around me rotated faster.

The rain seemed to fall harder.

The thunder grew louder.

I'm not a quitter, but I was losing.

Losing strength.

Losing consciousness.

Losing the fight.

Only one other thing I could do.

I screamed.

Above the continuous rhythm of the rainfall.

Above the thunder.

I screamed.

At the top of my lungs.

As water fell to the back of my throat.

I screamed.

Pleaded for help.

Someone had to hear me.

Someone had to be nearby.

Someone.

Anyone.

I screamed again.

And then he pressed his forearm against my throat.

My screaming stopped.

I was weak, but I continued to struggle, continued to fight.

As he pressed on my throat with one hand, he undid his pants and pulled his dick out with the other.

I continued to fight.

As he forced my legs apart, causing the skin of my ass to rip on the concrete.

I continued to fight.

As he took his dick and rammed it past the walls I tried desperately to keep closed.

I continued to fight.

As he slammed himself inside of me over and over and over and over again.

I continued to fight.

As he grunted and came and then pulled himself out of me and ran away.

I continued to fight.

And then I lay still, listening to the thunder and watching the lightning, while being drenched in the downpour, until the devil appeared above me and wrapped me in his arms.

Then I passed out.

23

Not the devil. Just a fat man named Jim.

That's who had wrapped his arms around me. He'd been on his way to his car when he noticed a half naked, bleeding, barely conscious woman, laying out in the rain. Had he left the gym ten minutes earlier . . .

Too little. Too late.

He rushed me in his car to the hospital and made sure I was seen right away. Fat Jim, the hero who saved the damsel in distress. He'd be larger than life and get his fifteen minutes on the eleven o'clock news and in the newspaper. After that, he'd go back to being just Fat Jim.

I was lucky. Had Fat Jim been a sadistic son of a bitch, he could have put me in his car and taken me somewhere and lived out some sick, demented sexual fantasy, and then done away with my body. But Fat Jim wasn't sick, and instead of taking me deep into the woods, or to a run down, foul-smelling apartment, littered with boxes of half-eaten fast food with roaches crawling through and over them, he took me to the hospital. I guess he doesn't deserve to be called Fat Jim.

I had barely been conscious when he carried me into the E.R. I'd been slipping in and out ever since he'd taken me out of the rain. I saw, felt and heard nothing as the doctors and nurses examined me, yet I saw, felt and heard it all at the same time. People in scrubs appearing, disappearing, and then reappearing around me. The prodding, the pressing. The questions, random, varied, repetitive and personal. Everything moved in and out of focus. Became loud and then silent.

It was surreal, yet I understood that what was happening and what had happened was all too real.

The rain. The thunder. The lightning. The man dressed in black with gloves like O.J. The hits. The punches. The kicks. The forearm against my throat. The dick being forced inside of me. The cum being spilled.

I had been raped.

By the man in black.

By Kyra.

Then by the doctors who were all simply just doing their jobs.

Sometime after the prodding, the stitching, the blood being drawn, the medication being given, and the questions I wouldn't answer, I passed out again.

When I woke up, Marlene was there, sitting in a chair beside me, snoring lightly. It hurt, but I moved slightly. With my movement, Marlene's eyes snapped open.

She rose from the chair and put her hand on my shoulder. "Hey there," she said softly.

I looked toward the window and stared at dust floating through the rays of sunlight. I had a bitter taste in my mouth. I said, "I need something to drink."

"Water or juice?"

"Juice."

"I'll be right back."

Marlene left and returned a few minutes later with a cup of apple juice. I winced as I pressed the button on the side-rail to rise to sit up a bit.

After taking a slow sip of juice, which wasn't easy to do with the swelling and stitches in the corner of my bottom lip, I asked, "How did you know I was here?"

Marlene sighed and then looked away from me to the window. When she looked back at me, her eyes had welled with tears. "Kyra called my cell two nights ago and . . . and said that I should check on you. She didn't say anything else and hung up before I could say anything. I called you right away on both of your cell phones and your home phone, but I kept getting your voice mails." She paused and wiped tears away from the corners of her eyes. "I'm so sorry, Lisette. It . . . it was raining so hard that night. I didn't have anyone to watch Ben, and I didn't want to take him out into the storm, so I waited until the next day to go to your condo.

"I was knocking on your door when two police officers—detectives—approached me and started bombarding me with questions. What was my name, why was I there, how did I know you, when was the last time I'd seen you? It wasn't easy, but I managed to convince them that I was a friend, and then I got them to tell me what had happened to you. I rushed over here right away. Lisette . . .

I . . . I'm so sorry," she said again, her voice trailing off. As she wiped more tears from her eyes, I leaned my head back against the pillow and closed my eyes for a moment.

Friend.

I'd never really associated that word with anyone in my life before. Growing up as an only child,
I'd never had to share my time or my possessions,
so sharing and giving of myself was just something I never connected with. From childhood,
through my teenage years to adulthood, that dis-
connection never changed. I never let anyone in
because I never felt the need to.

Friend.

I don't know that I'd ever give anyone that title
completely, but if I had to give it to someone,
Marlene was the closest to being just that. Her
concern was genuine, and on some level, I actually appreciated it. But at the same time, I still
wished that when I opened my eyes, she would
have been gone. It was hard enough for me having to deal internally with what had happened.
The tears, the pathetic pity in her voice—Marlene's presence was just too fucking much for
me.

I was a victim again.

Damn it.

I was a victim.

Again.

Behind my closed eyelids, the man in the
black ski mask winked at me. I opened my eyes

my quickly. Marlene was still there. Still wiping tears.

She said, "The police . . . they said that you're not talking to them. Is that true?"

I nodded.

"But why? Don't you want to tell them that Kyra had this done to you?"

"I have no proof, Marlene."

"But she called my cell phone."

"Did you record the conversation?"

"No."

"Then the call doesn't mean anything."

"But—"

"But nothing, Marlene. Without that call, or anything else, I have nothing."

Marlene sighed and walked over to the window. "This isn't fair," she said, her voice choking up. "What she did . . . I just can't believe she's going to get away with this. She can't get away with it. There's got to be something we can do."

"We?"

I had been trying to stay calm. Trying to ride out her genuine sympathy. But the questions, the insistence, and finally the word just made it too fucking impossible. We.

"What are you talking about, Marlene? There is no we!"

"But Lisette . . ."

"Please, just shut the fuck up! I was the one laying on the ground, not you! There is no we! You don't have to do anything but get the fuck out of here. Now!"

Marlene's eyes were wide as she stammered. "Lisette . . . I . . . I didn't mean—"

"Get the fuck out!" I snapped again.

I hadn't meant for my words to be so callous, so cruel, but she wouldn't shut up, and that, along with the pity in her eyes, and the vivid scenes from the parking lot running through my mind, made my words and the feelings behind them fire. I wanted her gone. I wanted to be alone. I needed to be alone. I was a victim again.

My heart raced. My head throbbed. My insides hurt from the tension and the outburst.

"Get the fuck out!"

Victim.

That word. The man in black. Kyra. The thunder. The rain. I tried to fight it. Tried to regain my composure. But it was too much for me. I was losing it. My eyes were welling with tears. I couldn't catch my breath.

Victim.

The room began to spin.

Rain began to pour.

I was being drenched again.

"Get out!"

Someone grabbed me.

Pushed me down.

Pinned me.

One, two, three people around me.

Dressed in black.

Winking.

Laughing.

Kyra sends her regards.

I screamed. Tears erupted from my eyes. Something stuck me in my arm. Seconds later the spinning went from a hare's to a tortoise's pace. The people around me faded in and out. Their outfits changed from black to teal. The tortoise's pace became a snail's. I tried to fight. Tried to run away. But I couldn't. Just as I had in the parking lot, beneath the downpour, I lost. My eyes closed.

Later that night, something stuck me in the arm, and I lost again.

24

A dream.

A very bad one.

That was the only way to describe what I was seeing.

Kyra. The moon glowing behind her. She was wearing scrubs. Looking down at me.

I closed my eyes and then opened them. She was still there. Still staring. I closed and opened them again. The nightmare was still occurring.

I tried to sit up. When I did, everything swooned. I felt like I was on a boat, careening from side to side in the middle of the ocean, in the midst of the perfect storm.

Kyra said, "If I were you, I'd lay still. Moving only makes it worse."

I opened my mouth, or at least it felt like I did, and said, "W—what did . . . y—you . . . do to me?" I couldn't be sure, but I think saliva was dripping from the corner of my mouth and down my chin.

"I gave you something to help you relax."

I tried to sit up again, but the boat careened and nearly capsized. My stomach twisted. I felt as though I were about to throw up.

"I heard about what happened to you," Kyra said. "I rushed over as soon as I could."

"B—bitch," I said, or slurred. "You . . . bitch." I couldn't see or think straight. Whatever she'd given me was potent. Hopefully not lethal.

"Is that any way to talk to a concerned friend?"

"Y-you won't . . . won't get away with th—this." Three Kyras smiled at me. I tried, but couldn't focus them into one. My heart beat heavily and quickly, as though I'd taken speed. "I won't . . . won't let you . . . get away with thi—this."

The three Kyras laughed. Together their voices created a demonic echo. "What are you going to do, Lisette? Go to the police with all of the proof you have? Or maybe run to Myles again? Bitch. You really thought you had gotten over on me, didn't you? You really thought that by telling Myles that, I was going to be screwed? Well, guess what, bitch? You didn't accomplish any-thing."

The three Kyras walked slowly around from one side of the bed to the other, tracing a finger over my body the entire time. I wanted to call out for a nurse, but couldn't find my voice or the strength to do it.

"See, after you turned my offer down, I took matters into my own hands, by fucking the only man my husband has been trying to get into bed with. Charles Goodell, or Chuckie, as he likes for me to call him. Besides Donald Trump, Chuckie is the only other major player in the real estate game. He owns several key blocks of property in Manhattan and Harlem, along with some property along the Vegas strip that Trump has been trying to take from him for years. Myles, of course, wants the property in Harlem."

"For months he's been trying to get into bed with Chuckie, and for months he's gotten nowhere. Chuckie's from the old school. Grew up when Whites owned the front of the bus and the word *nigger* wasn't a term of endearment. He understands the world has changed, but he can't pull away from the times that shaped him into the success that he became.

"That's why he'd turned down numerous offers from Myles to partner with him. Despite the millions that he'd acquire from tapping into the darker side of the force, he just couldn't see himself calling a black man his equal. But . . ." The three Kyras paused, tapped several fingers on the bed's side rail, and then said, "Chuckie had a secret."

The Kyras smiled as heavy rhythms reverberated in my head, and the room and the bed I lay on shook, rattled and rolled. My stomach twisted into knots. I struggled to focus, think, speak, and move. What the hell had she done to me? The Kyras moved from the foot of the bed to the top. I could barely turn to look at them.

They smiled devilishly and put their hands on my forehead. They leaned forward, said, "Awww, you poor, pathetic bitch," and then pressed their lips hard down against my wounded mouth.

However sluggish it was, I squirmed and moaned from the pressure and pain as they forced their tongue past my stitched lips into my mouth. Seconds passed before they pulled away and stared down at me with another maliciously blurred smile.

I tried to call out for help, but my cry was low and muffled, as though I was still being French kissed. I tried to move again, but the effects of whatever she had given me had gotten stronger and everything was just moving too much for me to move with it.

I lay still.

I rose and fell with the crests of the tumultuous waves around me.

I spun off axis.

My heart beat so hard and fast, I couldn't catch my breath.

Where the hell were the nurses that had been checking on me for what seemed like every fifteen minutes? Where the hell were the doctors? The police with their questions? Where was Marlene with her overbearing sentiment?

As everything rocked from side to side and back and forth, the Kyras said, "Chuckie has a thing for black pussy. That's his secret. I figured that out when Myles introduced me to him at a business function. I could tell by the animalistic way he looked at me. You see, bitch, you're not the only one that knows how to use what they have. I seduced the shit out of Chuckie, and made him eat whatever the fuck I was serving from the palm of my hands. By the time I was done with him, I had him telling Myles that after running into me in a café and listening to me explain how beneficial and lucrative a partnership with my husband would be, he saw no reason not to make the deal happen. And guess what? That's exactly what happened.

"So you see, whore, because I played a major part in adding to my husband's wealth, I negated his ridiculous prenup. He can't just walk away from this marriage without giving me a very nice piece of the pie."

Despite the dizziness, I shook my head. I said, "If . . . you had a plan already . . . w—why? Why . . . did you do . . . this to . . . me? You . . . didn't have . . . to . . . do . . . this."

The Kyras closed their eyes a fraction. "Because you thought you were just too damned good. Arrogant bitch. Guess I showed you, huh?" Without saying another word, Kyra turned and left the room.

Anxiety came over me as I struggled to catch a breath.

My heart raced. I felt feverish and cold at the same time. Kyra and the man in black. They laughed at me as my tears fell. I'd become a victim again, and it had all been for nothing. She'd had a plan. None of this had to happen. They laughed. I cried. And then the perfect storm took me under.

25

I'd never been broken before. Not when my father fucked me visually as a teenager. Not when my mother abandoned me and left me alone with his perverted ass. Not even when my ex-boyfriend tried everything in his power to break me. He'd come close, but all he'd gotten for his effort was a permanent residence in a pine box.

Never broken.

I was superhuman without the bulletproof skin and the heat vision. My movements were unmatched without having to move faster than the speed of light. I'd never tried to leap over a building in a single bound, but make no mistake, had there been a building blocking my path, I would have found a way to scale it by miles.

I was just always that good.

I was always unbreakable.

And then my Kryptonite called me and made me an offer I chose to refuse, and my reality had been distorted ever since.

Three weeks after Kyra's hospital visit, I sat in my apartment, cracked and on the verge of shattering into pieces. I'd become a paranoid wreck, jumping and cringing to sounds out in the hallway. I was barely eating, and barely sleeping, thanks to the NoDoz I was popping in my mouth every couple of hours to avoid the nightmares I'd been having of the man in the black ski mask beating me down and raping me while Kyra stood off to the side, watching it happen, laughing hysterically.

Sometimes the nightmares were worse. Sometimes there was more than one man in black. Other times, Kyra joined in and beat me down while the men in black held me down. In those nightmares, she helped keep my legs apart while they each took a turn sending her regards.

Kyra.

She'd done what no one had been able to do. She'd broken me and turned me into the type of woman I couldn't stand. The type of woman I swore I'd never be like.

Unsure.

Afraid.

Weak.

I couldn't handle it. With each passing moment of the solitude I'd thrown myself into, I lost myself more and more, and had it not been for Marlene and her insistence that we were friends, I would have disappeared entirely and never gotten Kyra back for what she'd done. But I did get Kyra back, and I would always be indebted to Marlene for forcing me to accept her as that.

Despite my meltdown and blowup at her in the hospital, Marlene refused to do what I wouldn't have given a second thought about doing—give up on me. She called me numerous times on both of my Sidekicks, and even though I wouldn't return the calls, she still left countless messages. Over the three week period, she came to my apartment and knocked on my door incessantly and begged me to let her in to talk. I never answered her, though. I just sat and listened, and wished for her to go away and not come back. At the same time, however, I also wished for her to continue knocking, because as much as I wanted to be left alone, there was a sense of security I felt knowing that she was there on the other side of the door.

Three times she'd come by, three times I'd refused to open the door or even respond, and three times she'd given up and left. I expected the same scenario to happen for her fourth visit.

I was organizing my walk-in closet in my bedroom when she came knocking. My closet wasn't cluttered with any unnecessary things, or outfits that were hanging taking up space needlessly. Actually, it was already neat, with clothes and shoes and whatever odds and ends I had in there all systematically lined up. My reason for being in there was strictly to keep myself busy. Cleaning things that didn't need to be cleaned. Arranging things that were already well arranged. Reconfiguring rooms that already had the furniture sitting in the perfect spot, in the perfect position. That's what I'd been doing during my weeks of solitude. Whatever I could do to occupy my mind and my time, I did. The walk-in was the last of the busywork I had left to do. Once I finished that, I planned to move on to dusting my light fixtures, and maybe even breaking my toaster just to try to fix it.

Marlene was just supposed to knock a few times, call out my name, call my phones, call my name again, knock a few more times, and then finally give up and leave me to finish doing what I was doing.

She wasn't supposed to knock and say, "I'm not leaving this time, Lisette. Ben is with the babysitter and she'll watch him all night if I need her to. And if I need her longer than that, it won't be a problem. So you see . . . I'm not going anywhere. I'm going to stay here and knock until you open the door and let me inside, or you call the police and have me taken away. It's your choice, Lisette."

I sighed, dropped a pile of clothes I had in my arms on my bed, and walked to the living room. I could ignore her all I wanted, but the fact was she wasn't going to leave. There was a conviction in her voice that hadn't been there before. A no nonsense, no bullshit tone.

I sighed again and went to the door, and said, "The police will be here in five minutes."

Marlene said, "Open the door, Lisette."

I shook my head. "Your calls aren't answered, your messages aren't returned, the door is never opened. Don't you know how to take a hint?"

"Open the door, Lisette."

"No."

"Then call the police."

"Like I said, they'll be here in five minutes."

"Then I'll wait for them."

Another sigh. "Why are you here, Marlene?"

"Because whether you want to accept it or not, I'm your friend."

"I don't need friends."

"Of course you don't."

"Then you can leave."

"That's not going to happen. Not this time."

"I'm not going to open the door," I said defiantly.

"Then call the police, Lisette."

I clenched my jaws. Bumps rose on my skin. A lump had formed in my throat. Tears that I hadn't shed since Kyra's visit were trying to well in my eyes. I closed them tightly. I couldn't cry. Not again.

"Can you just leave, Marlene?"

"No. I can't."

I took a deep breath. Let it out slowly. I wanted to ask her to leave again. Wanted to demand it. But I knew there was no point to it. I put my hand on the top lock. Gave serious consideration to calling the police. Then turned the lock counterclockwise, wrapped my fingers around the doorknob, turned and pulled the door open.

I looked at Marlene as she stared back at me. "Are you happy now?"

She smiled. Said, "Yes." And then said, "You look like shit."

I closed my eyes a bit. "It's not too late for me to call the police, you know."

Marlene smiled.

For the first time in weeks, I did too.

I said that I didn't need any friends, but standing there in front of Marlene, I realized just how much I'd been lying to myself.

I stepped back and opened the door wide. Marlene walked past me. "So how have you been?"

I closed the door and turned around. "I've been fine."

Marlene frowned and gave me a look filled with skepticism. "You have dark circles under your eyes and you look like you've lost a little weight, which means that you haven't been eating or sleeping much. Don't tell me that you're fine."

"How about great? Peachy. Never better," I said, walking into the living room.

Marlene followed behind me. "Damn it, Lisette! I'm your friend! Will it kill you to open up to me just once?"

"What do you want me to say?"

"Tell me how you're really feeling!"

"What do you want to hear, Marlene? That I haven't been sleeping because I've been popping NoDoz like candy to keep from having nightmares? That I haven't had the desire to eat? That I've been locked up in my apartment for the past three weeks, cleaning it from top to bottom, arranging and rearranging over and over again just to keep my mind off of the fact that that bitch had me beaten and raped? That she came to visit me in the hospital, she drugged me, and then told me how none of what had happened to me had been necessary because she figured out a way to get her fucking money anyway?

"Is that good enough for you, Marlene? Do you feel better now? Does it give you satisfaction knowing that I feel weak, broken, humiliated, and pathetic? Does that work for you? Is this better than seeing me break down, held down and then sedated? Did I share enough of my fucking feeling with you, *friend*?"

I stopped ranting and stared at Marlene. I was breathing heavily as though I'd been running laps for hours. My heart was racing. My hands were balled at my sides. I hadn't meant to go off that way. Hadn't meant to lose my composure and reveal so much. Hadn't meant to reveal anything, actually. But the pain, frustration, embarrassment, resentment, anger, hatred, and rage I'd been suppressing refused to stay down any longer, and before I could keep it from happening, the words just exploded out of me.

For a few seconds Marlene just stared at me with an expression of shock, concern, and pity. The shock and concern I could deal with. The pity just annoyed me. I shook my head and frowned, and regretted my outburst.

Marlene looked at me for a few more seconds, and then finally verbalized what she'd been saying with her eyes. "Lisette . . . I had no idea. I'm so sorry."

I should have said that she had nothing to apologize for. That it hadn't been her fault. Instead I said, "Being sorry doesn't change what happened."

"Why didn't you come to me?"

"Come to you for what, Marlene?"

"We could have talked sooner."

"Talked sooner? I don't even want to talk now."

"Sometimes talking about things can really help."

"Would talking erase what happened?"

"No, but—"

"Then to hell with the talking, Marlene. Shit!" I passed my hand through my hair and then clasped it down around the back of my neck. Said, "Shit!" again and exhaled.

Marlene stared at me. Didn't say a word. Just stared. There was something about the way she was watching me that bothered me. Made me feel . . . self-conscious. It wasn't a look she'd ever given me before.

It made me say, "What?"

She shook her head and smirked a little. "Unbelievable," she said, her voiced peppered with disgust.

"What's unbelievable?"

"I came to talk to Lisette, and instead, I end up wasting my time with you."

"Excuse me?"

"The real Lisette wouldn't have kept herself locked away, cowering in the shadows. The real Lisette would have never continued being the victim while some bitch, who isn't even in her league, walked around with her nose in the air, thinking that she'd won. The Lisette I know would have never, ever admitted to being weak or afraid. Do me a favor and please tell the real Lisette to come out of the bedroom, because you're a horrible carbon copy."

Marlene paused and looked at me.

I was stunned. First the look, and now she'd verbally chastised me. Challenged me. Called me out. Had everything she'd said not been so dead on, I would have been pissed. But I couldn't be, because she was right.

Who the hell was I?

I've never shied away from anything or anyone. If something or someone stood in my way, I made it my mission to crush whatever or whoever it was. I thrived on breaking things down. Especially people. I reveled in breaking a person's spirit. I didn't care if they were a man or a woman. If in any way, shape, or form, they tried to have the upper hand, I showed them very quickly that there was no getting over on me.

Domination and control.

Two words that personified my character.

I'd given them up to Kyra. I let her dominate. I let her have control. I let her make me weak. Let her make me afraid. The real Lisette would never have allowed that to happen.

I looked at Marlene.

She was staring at me intensely as she said, "This bitch is nothing compared to you, Lisette. You know that."

I nodded. "I know."

"Then for Christ's sake, stop letting her win! She gave you her best shot and it wasn't good enough because you survived."

I nodded again. Felt more bumps rise from my skin. I survived. In my weeks alone, when I couldn't run away from the thoughts of everything that had happened, that was one phrase that never popped into my head.

I was beaten.

I was raped.

I was broken.

I was weak.

I was pathetic.

I was angry.

All of the phrases combined couldn't match the strength that phrase held. I'd been hit with her best shot, yet I was still breathing, still standing.

I survived.

I looked at Marlene. Thought about hugging her. Maybe even made a subtle move to do that. But then I held still.

She'd helped me through a period I would never let go. For that she would always be acknowledged as my friend, and I would always be indebted to her. But I was Lisette. And hugging wasn't what I did.

I looked at Marlene and said, "It's time to pay the bitch back."

Marlene smiled. "Welcome back."

26

Before I fucked up Kyra's world for good, there were a couple of things I wanted to take care of.

First, I went back to the gym. My reason for going there was two-fold. One, I needed to go back to the scene of the crime. I just needed to be there. I needed to come to terms with that night and all that had happened. It was part of my reality and I needed to face it, and embrace it and all of its horrible moments. I stood still and I looked up into the sky, squinting at the sun, and thought about the black and grey clouds, the thunder and lightning, and all of the rain that had fallen. I let the memory soak in like the rain. I was beaten. I was raped. Now I was standing where it all happened. Stronger. More determined than ever to demonstrate that I wasn't the one to be fucked with.

I closed my eyes as the sun shone down on me, and I listened to the silence in the sky. Somewhere above, a plane flew by, sounding like mock thunder. I listened to it and remembered the thunder from that night. Remembered the cracking of the lightning. Remembered the rain: cold, heavy, falling lead pellets. I lowered my head and looked down at the ground, where I'd been forced to take Kyra's regards. So much rain had fallen on me. I should have drowned. Would have had it not been for Fat Jim. I was back to having my me-and-fuck-everyone-else mentality, but I wasn't so caught up that I wasn't able to truly thank him for what he'd done for me, which was the second reason I'd gone back there. I took one last glance at the ground. My reality had changed, because on the ground, I was staring at myself smiling and being fucked instead of being violated.

I went into the gym. Fat Jim was on the second level, huffing and puffing his pounds off on the treadmill. I didn't remember much about him physically, but it almost seemed like he'd lost a few pounds. If he kept it up, I wouldn't be able to call him Fat Jim anymore.

When he saw me, he flashed one of the most attractive smiles I'd ever seen a man flash. With handsome, deep-set brown eyes, dimples, full lips, and smooth but sweaty cocoa-brown skin,

I actually wondered what the rest of the package would look like without the weight.

He came down off of the treadmill and attempted to give me a hug. I didn't mean to be so callous, but I stopped him by sticking out my hand. His smile dropped slightly as disappointment registered on his face, before he took my hand.

We went to the café on the first level of the gym and talked. He wanted to know how I had been doing. Told me that he'd been worried and had come to the hospital to see me the next day, but because I was a rape victim and they had no suspect and he wasn't next of kin, they wouldn't let him see me. He told me about the police questioning him and requesting a sample of his sperm, which he gave without hesitation. I told him I was fine and thanked him again for what he'd done. He insisted it had been no big deal. I told him that his insistence made it just that. Said in today's world, heroes were only seen on Mondays at nine. That most people would have said to hell with saving the world and just hurried to their car to get out of the rain. He said his father taught him to never ignore a woman. I said his father was a smart man.

We spoke for a few more minutes after that. He asked if I had any idea about who my attacker had been. I lied and said I didn't. He said it was a damn shame. That he wished he would have come out sooner. Said he would have kicked the guy's ass. I believed him and told him so. He apologized for showing up too late. I told him that he had been right on time. Then I gave him a gift.

I told him about a deal our company had signed with a new client, Bryant "Big Man" Drew. Considered to be one of the funniest black men in America, he was becoming very bankable in Hollywood, as his last two films had brought in over eighty million dollars each. Big Man was the male Monique, and at two hundred and fifty plus pounds, he was letting nothing stand in his way.

We'd just formed a partnership with Big Man to design a new clothing line for plus-sized men that would bear his moniker. I told Fat Jim that Big Man was on the hunt for male models to represent the line that was going to get major play in *Vibe*, *Essence*, *GQ*, and billboards around the country. Said that for everything he'd done, I told Bryant personally that I had his star model already. Then I presented Fat Jim with a contract, given to me by Big Man himself. Told him to have a lawyer look it over and then sign it and take it to Big Man's people. Said he could quit his day job. That the contract was a lucrative, life-changing one.

Fat Jim was speechless at first, and then eventually said that he didn't help me to get any type of reward. Then he tried to turn down my gift. I told him that turning it down was equivalent to leaving me out in the rain. Fat Jim nodded, asked for a pen and signed the contract right then and there.

A few more minutes after that, I left to take care of the other business on my agenda. But before I walked away, I did something that actually surprised me: I gave Fat Jim a hug. Then I told him not to lose too much weight. Fat Jim laughed, gave me another hug, thanked me for the gift, and called me a beautiful woman. I surprised myself again by giving him a kiss on the cheek. Then I left the gym. Fat Jim was a genuine, real, good man. Maybe one of the last ones left.

Unlike Steve, who I went to see next.

27

This time I visited his office. He was on his phone, his back to the door, staring out the window, talking to some woman, flirting.

I leaned against the inner doorframe and watched him and listened to him tell the female that he was skilled in a lot of areas. And how she wouldn't be disappointed and may even become hooked. I watched him without saying a word for a few minutes, until he swiveled around in his chair, made eye contact with me, and nearly gagged on his words. He told the female that he would call her back, and then hung up quickly without waiting for her response, and then stood up.

"Lisette! Wh . . . what are you doing here?"

I stepped into his office and closed the door behind me. I also locked it. I said, "That woman you were just talking to . . . does she know that you're a rapist?"

Steve's eyes grew wide. "Wh-what?"

The night Marlene helped bring me back from the nearly-dead, I dreamt about the night with the man in black. The rain, the thunder, the lightning. They were all present in Technicolor and surround sound. Like the other dreams I'd had, I relived the kicks, the punches, the pushes, the pulls. I slipped in the puddle, fell back, and cracked my skull on the ground. As the rain beat down on me, the man in black climbed on top of me and began to force my pants down. The nightmares were all the same. Building slowly to that awful climactic moment.

Only this time . . .

This night . . .

The dream was different. In all of the other dreams, I'd ignored the fact that I'd noticed something when the man in black was on top of me. A fragrance. Men's cologne. Contradiction for Men by Calvin Klein. I'd smelled it a few times before that night.

At Marlene's house during the dinner party.

In my office with a tongue inside of my pussy.

Back at Marlene's house, on the couch.

Steve's cologne.

I inhaled it when he was ramming himself into me. Despite the mask and the whispered regards, I knew who he was. I was just so caught up in being the victim again that I'd blocked away that moment and that smell from my mind.

I said, "Next time wear a different cologne, asshole."

Steve did a horrible job of feigning ignorance again. "What are you talking about? A rapist?"

"Cut the bullshit," I said, my skin getting warm.

Steve took a step back. He'd tried to make it subtle, but it had been awkward, shaky. "I don't know what you're . . . what you're talking about."

I took a step forward. My legs were wobbly too, but unlike Steve, it wasn't my nerves. They were shaking because they were itching to spring and pounce, but I was holding them back. "I know it was you, you son of a bitch! I smelled your fucking cologne."

Steve took another step back. A few more and he'd be pressing up against the window.

I stared at him. Fear was encompassing his body. Did I have a gun? A knife? Wire to wrap around his throat? His eyes wanted to know. I took another step toward him. Made him take another one back.

"You better leave. Now!"

I shook my head. "You fucking coward," I said, my tone sharper, my volume rising. "You don't have your mask to hide behind now, you fucking pussy!"

"You better leave, Lisette. I'm warning you."

I took another step forward. Caused him to stumble a little as he backed up again. His next step would put his back against the window. "You're warning me? Let *me* give *you* a warning, you cowardly piece of shit! You better listen and do what I tell you to do right now, or I will fuck up your life forever! Are you hearing me?"

"I don't . . . I don't know—"

"I said are you fucking hearing me!" I yelled out.

I didn't give a shit that it was midday. I didn't care that there were employees who had undoubtedly heard my outburst. The bastard had raped me. Nothing and no one was going to stop me from returning the favor.

"Do not say another fucking word, or I swear to God you will regret it."

There was a sudden knock on his office door. Then a female voice saying, "Steve? Is everything all right?"

Steve looked toward the door. Had salvation in his eyes.

I shook my head, lowered my voice, and said, "Tell her to leave."

Steve looked from me to the door. The door to me. My stare back at him was filled with malice, with promised intent.

He cleared his throat, kept his eyes on me, and said, "Everything's fine, Nancy."

Nancy said, "Are you sure?"

I shook my head in disgust and went to the door and opened it. "He's sure," I said, glaring at a twenty-something blond female.

Nancy looked at me as I stared at her. I looked at her. Dared her to give me lip. Was practically on the verge of begging her to. I was holding back on Steve, but I had no reason to for her. All she had to do was say something.

Behind me, Steve said, "Everything's fine, Nancy. We're just discussing some things."

Nancy looked over my shoulder at Steve. I kept my eyes locked on her. When she fixed her sights back on me, I said, "Goodbye, Nancy," and then I slammed the door shut in her face.

I locked the door again and went back to the desk. "You're a joke," I said. "Where's your fight now, you son of a bitch? You pathetic piece of shit. You should have killed me, asshole. You shouldn't have left me there. Now your ass is going to pay."

Steve's shoulders slouched down. "What do you want?" he asked, his tone riddled with defeat.

"What do I want?" I chuckled. "Do you mean besides wanting to ram something up your ass? Do you mean besides wanting to take a switch-blade and slice your dick off and then feed it to you? Is that what you mean?"

Steve remained silent and continued to look at me.

I moved forward and slammed my hand down on the top of his desk.

"Answer me, motherfucker! Is that what you mean?" I wanted to flip the desk out of my way, charge him, and do everything I'd just said. And more. But as hard as it was, I held back. I was there to pay him back, and hurting him physically, though tempting, wasn't good enough.

Steve nodded and said in a low, stressed-filled voice, "Y—yes."

I clenched my jaws and then grabbed a seat and sat down. Steve remained standing, afraid and unsure as to what I would do. At that moment, I wished I smoked. I would have lit a cigarette, taken a long drag on it, held the smoke deep in my lungs for a few seconds, and then blown it out slowly as my eyes remained locked on his.

I said, "So was it fun, Steve? Fucking me against my will. Fucking me while I was half conscious. Did you get a thrill? Did you feel better after you came inside of me? Did you feel like you'd gotten me back? Answer me, Steve. Did it make you feel powerful?"

Steve shook his head, then took his hand, put it over his forehead and squeezed his temples with his thumb and middle finger. He breathed out heavily. "I . . . I . . . I'm sorry," he said, his voice barely audible.

I passed my tongue over the front of my top teeth. "Fuck you and your apology," I said.

"I never meant for that to . . . to happen. I was only going to rough you up. I never planned on . . ." He paused. Looked up at the ceiling. Said, "Christ," and then squeezed his temples again. "I'm not a rapist." He shook his head and struggled with the truth. "I'm not a rapist," he said again.

"I just wanted to get you back for what you helped Marlene do to me."

I laughed. "For what we did to you? Asshole. How many times did you fuck around on Marlene? You say you're not a rapist, but you raped Marlene every time you couldn't keep your dick in your pants." I laughed again. "You're a fool, Steve. You got off easy with the divorce. A couple thousand a month, that's all you had to deal with. But now . . ."

I paused and sat forward.

"Now, you're fucked. I don't know whose plan it was, but you should have never gotten into bed with that bitch, because now you're going to be paying a hell of a lot more."

"Lisette—"

I put up my hand. "Shut. The. Fuck. Up."

He did.

"The police have a sperm sample on file, but guess what they don't have." I stopped talking and watched him intently. "They don't have a suspect to go with the sperm because I haven't given them any information. I wonder what would happen if I went to them and told them about how you had threatened to hurt me. What do you think would happen, Steve? Do you think they'd come and pay you a visit? Maybe start asking you questions? I guess you'd have an airtight alibi, huh? Someone or some people that could put you at another place at the same time."

"Maybe that could get you off the hook. Or maybe not. Maybe to get you off of their radar completely, they would ask you to submit a sperm sample. What then, Steve? Do you decline to give it, thereby staying high on their radar, forcing them to get a court order making you give one? Do you voluntarily give it and then pray for the mother of all miracles that somehow your sample ends up getting lost? Or maybe you just leave town and go into hiding somewhere, hoping they'll just forget about you someday. Do you see where I'm going with this?"

Steve watched me for several long, tense seconds. Stress had his shoulders lower than before. Fear and anxiety had his forehead knotted up.

"The worst thing you can go to jail for is pedophilia or rape. Even criminals, as immoral as they can be, have morals, and they consider those crimes to be two of the most cowardly that a man can do. You really don't want to be locked up for either of those crimes, because you can be sure someone will be out to get you."

I stopped talking and sat back in the chair. I watched him. Watched him breathe. Watched him think. Watched him digest everything I'd just said. I held his life in my hands. Like I'd told him, he would have been better off killing me and dumping my body somewhere.

"What will it take?" he asked.

"How valuable is your freedom, you piece of shit? How valuable is your reputation?"

"What will it take, Lisette?"

I looked at him. Thought about going Lorena Bobbitt on him with the box cutter I had in my purse.

What would it take?

I said, "Fifty thousand dollars a month."

His mouth fell open. "Fifty thous . . . that's six hundred thousand dollars a year."

"You're good at math."

"That's . . . that's insane."

"No. That's what it would take for you to not spend the next fifty years of your life in jail."

"Six hundred thousand dollars a year," he repeated.

"You're an investment banker. You can afford it."

He squeezed his temples again and collapsed into his chair. He stretched his hands out on the top of his desk, his palms open and facing upward. "Is there anything else? Can we make another arrangement?"

"No."

"I'm sorry, Lisette. You've got to believe me. That night . . . that wasn't really me."

I said, "In prison, if they don't kill you, they'll end up making you somebody's bitch. How would you like that? How would you like to be forced to suck on another man's dick? How would you like to be the one taking it up the ass?"

"There's got to be something else," he said, shaking his head.

I stood up. "No. There isn't."

I turned to leave. Before I'd taken three steps, Steve said, "Okay."

I turned back around. "Okay, what?"

"I . . . I can't go to jail. I just can't."

"Okay, what?" I said again.

"I hate you, Lisette. I fucking hate you, bitch."

I said again, "Okay, what?"

"Fifty thousand a month. But I want it in writing that the figure won't change."

I gave him a look that said *nigga, please.* "You get nothing," I said.

"Bitch!" Steve spat, his hands balled into fists.

I looked down at him and laughed. Then said, "I want a check now."

28

Starbucks.

Seven-thirty in the morning.

The routine remained the same.

I sipped on a vanilla latte, grande size, and watched Myles walk into the café, his laptop in hand. I was sitting toward the back. Not by choice. That morning, everyone decided to get their caffeine fix at the exact same time. One lone table in the back had been my only option. I didn't mind. It gave me some time to sip and observe.

Myles looked left and then right, searching for an open table. He never looked in my direction. On his left, a young couple with book bags in their hands and sandals on their feet stood up and offered Myles their table. He thanked them and when they walked away, he set his laptop and his keys down and went to the line to get his own fix. For a brief moment, I thought about going and grabbing his laptop and leaving just to fuck up his routine. But I didn't.

I sipped.

I stared.

I scowled.

A few minutes later, Myles came back with his java, sat down and opened his laptop and began typing. I scowled as I looked at him and thought about walking over to him and spilling my latte all over the laptop. Steve was a piece of shit, but Myles was worse, because he was a poor excuse for a man.

I sipped my latte. Squeezed the sides of the cheap cup designed to let the liquid go cool within minutes. Thought again about short circuiting his laptop and then pouring some in his crotch.

I sipped.

I stared.

I scowled.

And then I stood up.

I walked over to him and stood off to his right side. My latte was in my hand, itching to be set free. What a waste. Aside from the fucking, he was useless. Any man without a backbone was.

I cleared my throat and said, "You're a pussy."

Myles looked up and saw me. "Lisette?"

I said, "You're a pussy," again.

His eyeballs darted from left to right to see who else had heard me. I didn't care about other eyes or ears.

He cleared his throat, closed his laptop, which had been a good thing to do considering the fact that I was seconds away from drowning his keyboard, and said, "Would you mind lowering your voice?"

I stared at him. He disgusted me. Steve had disgusted me too, but unlike Myles, Steve was allowing things in his life to be dictated because he had no choice. The judge decreed the amount he had to pay Marlene in child support each month. I decreed how much he had to pay me to stay out of jail. No choice. No other options. His back wasn't against the wall; it was being pressed through it. He was a pussy too, but he was a pussy because he was an ass. Myles was a pussy because, unlike Steve, he'd had a choice.

"You're pathetic," I said.

Myles cleared his throat again. Gave a smile to an older woman sitting at a table across from him reading a Jackie Collins novel. Then looked up at me. "Can you sit down, please?" he said, his voice low, tight with irritation.

I looked at him for a few seconds. He was so uncomfortable with me standing there. So conscious of others around him. I sat down, but not because he asked, and not because I cared.

He asked, "I haven't seen or spoken to you since the hotel. Is there a particular reason for the hostility?"

I stared at him but didn't respond right away. He had no clue about what had happened to me. No idea that that bitch was capable of much more than selling him on a lie. Part of my anger toward him was because I knew what she had been capable of. It didn't matter that he was in the dark. After our last conversation, he should have known better.

"You're staying with her because she helped get you into bed with Charles Goodell."

His head snapped back a little. "How did you know about that?"

"You're a waste of a man," I said, ignoring his question. "You don't deserve the dick you have."

His eyes darted from right to left again, and then he looked past me. Behind me, the woman cleared her throat, and said softly, "My word."

Myles didn't flash a smile this time. "So what else did she tell you?"

"Enough to know how much of a pussy you are."

Myles clenched his jaws. My words, my tone, my volume . . . they were pissing him off. I cut my eyes at him. Dared him to try to be a man with me.

He said, "You haven't heard my side of this."

"I don't need to hear your side. You sacrificed your manhood for a few dollars."

"Being partners with Charles is going to give me just a little more than a few dollars," he said.

"Fuck you and fuck Charles Goodell, or Chuckie, as she likes to call him when she's sucking his withered dick."

Myles' pupils widened as the woman behind me cleared her throat again.

I shook my head. "You didn't really believe that bullshit story she and Chuckie gave you about her convincing him over coffee that partnering with you was what was best for him, did you? You didn't really buy into believing that a man who's been a bigot all of his life, a man who'd turned you down numerous times before, had suddenly seen the light because of anything that bitch had to say, right? You're not that stupid to think that she wasn't fucking him, are you?"

Myles' chin dropped slightly as he stammered, "I . . . I had a feeling that there may have been something going on."

"You had a feeling?"

Myles looked at me and sighed. "Charles had been turning me down for over six months. Then all of a sudden, a month after I confront Kyra about trying to have me set up, Charles calls me out of the blue and tells me that he'd like to do business with me." He paused and laughed, and then continued. "He tells me all about how after having coffee with my *lovely wife*, he's now convinced that partnering with me would be lucrative for the both of us. That she helped him see how tapping into the minority market was the smartest thing for him to do.

"Am I that naïve to think that she hadn't gotten to him somehow? No. Did I think that she'd resort to fucking him? No. But after what she was trying to have you do to me, I gather she's capable of anything."

I raised an eyebrow, said, "So what happened to you hating her?"

"I still do."

"Then why are you forfeiting millions to her? Because you realize after getting into bed with Chuckie and allowing him to give her credit for your partnership, that no matter what you try to do, she's going to leave you and take much more than five million dollars."

Myles nodded. "I know."

"Then why partner with Chuckie?"

Myles sighed again. "I have a gambling problem. I've had it for years. Since my senior year in high school. It was recreational fun at first. I'd throw down a couple of twenties on college basketball and football games. NBA and NFL games. I'd win some and lose some, and not give it much thought. I had a job, I had no responsibilities. What the hell, right? In college the amounts I bet went from being a few twenties to a few hundred. I'd bet in several different pools, on and off campus. Winning meant extra money for food, clothes and partying. Losing just fueled the desire to win again.

"After college, the betting became more intense, as the few hundreds turned into thousands. I became addicted and compulsive, betting on anything that could have money placed on it. Professional and college game. Horse racing, golf, baseball, bowling, pool, etc. I couldn't get enough. It was like a drug. Hell, it is a drug. And the high from winning was euphoric and was even more addictive than the cash I won. It far outweighed the lows of losing the tens, twenties, hundreds, thousands, and tens of thousands, and eventually millions that I would lose more often than win.

"As the years have passed and my bank account became thicker, the stakes of bets became larger. I'd bet jewelry, vehicles, and eventually, when the money wasn't enough, the properties I owned. I couldn't stop myself. I tried. Shit . . . believe me . . . I tried. I'd go for days not placing a bet on something and I'd think okay, I'm conquering this thing. But then a big game would come up and the pull would be too strong, and I'd be back on the horse, betting my life and my possessions away again."

He paused and filled his lungs with java-flavored air and exhaled slowly. Frustration and shame dragged the corners of his mouth down.

"Getting into bed with Charles has saved me from being bankrupt. I've reaped the benefits by acquiring clientele from the circles that would have never dealt with me before Charles. It's only been a month, but I've actually been able to pay off some of my debt. I hate Kyra. Believe me. I hate her with a passion. But, whether I like her or not, she literally saved me."

Myles stopped talking and looked off to the side, refusing to make eye contact with me. Embarrassment draped an arm over his shoulder and gave him a reassuring squeeze.

I tapped my index finger on the table top and watched him.

The power of addiction.

People lost friends, family, homes, souls, lives, and their minds because of it. Being an addict meant being controlled. Being controlled meant someone or something was running the show. Being an addict meant you were weak, easily manipulated. I admired addiction and the power it possessed.

I watched Myles struggle to deal with his shame and shook my head. He was an idiot. He'd given Kyra everything she wanted because he was hooked on gambling not for money, but instead for a useless euphoric feeling. A feeling that would disappear just as quickly as it came.

I said, "Your laptop . . . what are you doing on it?"

Myles sighed. "Checking scores and placing bets."

I stared at him but didn't say anything. I didn't have to. The look on his face said it all.

He was pathetic.

Chuckie had saved him only so that he could drown himself and take Chuckie down with him another day. Because that was most certainly going to happen. And while water filled their lungs and caused them excruciating pain, Kyra would drift by them in a life raft filled with their money.

Of course, that would be until I caught up with her.

Myles grabbed his cup of coffee, took a sip and then groaned. The cheap cup conspiracy had gotten him. He looked at me. "I'm going to get another. Do you want anything?"

"No."

"Will you be here when I get back?"

"No."

He frowned. Said, "Okay," and then got up and walked away, leaving me alone with his laptop.

I looked at it.

It looked at me.

Said, *hello.*

Asked if I'd like to place a bet.

I thought about Myles, sitting in Starbucks each morning, pretending to work, but instead wasting his life away, masturbating with his bookie.

I grabbed the laptop, walked out of Starbucks and approached the curb. The city was alive with rush hour activity. I turned and looked back into Starbucks. Saw Myles approach his table and flip out when he noticed the laptop missing. I tossed the laptop into the middle of the street and walked.

Behind me, tires screeched.

The laptop shattered.

Myles screamed, "Shit!"

I walked.

I had one more person to deal with.

Six Months Later

29

40/40 Club.

Sitting at the bar.

Sipping on a passion 'n pagne.

Music was blasting the latest song by Beyoncé through the speakers. Celebrities, wannabes, groupies, and those just wanting to be seen filled the club's space. Some stood around and stared up at the sixty-inch plasma televisions, watching the video for the song being played. Some stood around and mingled. Some were out on the floor, moving to the infectious groove. The majority profiled, which is what the night was really all about anyway.

It was the release party for Beyoncé's new CD, and anyone who was anyone was there. NBA stars. NFL MVPs. Movie stars, young and old. Of course, the music elite were well represented. Country singers you'd never expect to see. R&B kings and queens. R&B princes and princesses.

Rap stars, old school and new. Jazz musicians. Pop stars gone wild. The star of the evening herself was there, sitting off in a VIP room with Jay-Z and a few other important people. Like I said—anyone who was anyone. Each trying to outdo the other in look and attitude.

I watched it all, yet I wasn't paying attention to any of it. My focus was on two people only. They were across from me in the far corner of the room. A man and a woman. Her back was flat against the wall, her arms draped over his shoulders. He was facing her, his back to me, pressing his crotch against her. They were kissing and gyrating to the beat sometimes. Other times they were dry humping to another beat altogether.

I'd been watching them for over an hour. The man was well aware of my presence and was making sure to put on one hell of a show, showing me that my money had been well spent. The woman had no clue I was there.

It wasn't easy, but I waited. Sat in my low cut black dress, sipped my passion 'n pagne, turned down one celebrity advance after another, and stuck to the plan I'd devised. It was probably one of the hardest things I'd had to do in a long time.

Wait.

Let everything unfold.

My plan.

My revenge.

Beyoncé's song ended and the latest gimmick rap sensation came on. Everyone on the floor began doing the same dance, popping to the side while snapping their fingers in the air. Like I'd said before—crap. I hated gimmick rap.

I looked past the snappers on the floor to my couple again. In another twenty minutes, he was going to lead her by the hand through the crowd on the dance floor, and pass me by the bar. She'd never notice me sitting there staring at her because the Ecstasy pills I'd had him slipping into her drinks would be running rampant through her system. She'd barely be able to focus on the steps she was taking. She'd barely be able to think past the sex that would be on her mind, from all the things I'd told him to say to her.

Nasty things he'd promised to do.

Positions he'd have her in.

Multiple orgasms he'd make her have.

She was going to love his dick.

He was going to make her call out his name.

She was never going to forget having him inside of her.

I watched them.

Watched her smile as he whispered the script in her ear. She was drunk, high.

Twenty minutes later, they walked by. I sipped my drink. Watched her. Saw the lust in her half-glazed eyes.

I followed behind a few minutes later. Staying several feet behind them, I watched him lead her to the car I'd given him to use. I listened to her laugh. Listened to her say how she wanted to give him a blow job in the car. I was parked behind them. She was so gone, she never even noticed me standing beside my door, watching them drive off.

I followed them to a condominium I'd purchased at The Exchange at 25 Broad Street. It was an elegant condo just a block away from the New York Stock Exchange. I'd had him tell her all about it before the Ecstasy. Had him describe the nine- to thirteen-foot ceilings. The marble-floored bathroom with glass wall tiling. Made sure he told her that at seven hundred and sixty-five thousand dollars, it had been a steal. I knew she'd be impressed. His stock, already high from his devilishly good looks and muscular frame, would rise by leaps and bounds after he made it appear as though money had been no object for him.

As instructed, he parked the car in the garage himself. I let the valet take my car and went into the lobby. They walked in minutes later.

She couldn't stand it. The alcohol, the Ecstasy, the promises to devour her . . . she was practically clawing at him as they stepped into the elevator. When the elevator doors closed behind them, I went to the bar and ordered a drink, and then I went upstairs.

I leaned against the inside of the bedroom doorframe and watched him fucking her from behind. She was holding onto the headboard, screaming, telling him how good he felt. Telling him how good his dick was. She'd never heard me walk into the condo.

She called out his name.

Called out to God.

Told him to fuck the shit out of her.

He pulled backward, thrust forward. Each time harder than the last. Made her moan. Made her "oooh."

I watched. Waited. Enjoyed. Not the sex, but her pleasure before the pain.

He changed positions, and keeping her back to me, sat her down on him. She gasped as he drove his dick up into her. She squealed and cursed. It was everything he'd promised.

Her pleasure guided my hand beneath my dress.
Made my finger slide past my thong. I massaged
my clit to the rhythm of their fucking. He fucked
her and watched me masturbate. This was a bonus
for a job well done.

My finger moved as they moved.

In and out.

Around, in circles.

She came.

I came.

This was the best sex we'd both had in a long
time.

And then everything changed.

He lashed out and punched her viciously in
the side of her head, sending her flailing off of
him and crashing to the floor, where she looked
up and saw me standing there.

Before she could process anything, he moved
on top of her, covered her mouth with duct tape,
and punched her over and over again. He broke
her nose, split her lip, hit her in her mid-section
so hard, I heard a rib break. She tried to fight,
but the ecstasy had her sluggish. She screamed
muffled screams and fought until she couldn't
anymore.

He fucked her again as she lay unmoving, on
the verge of passing out from the combination

of shock and pain. Then two men came from behind me and went and fucked her too.

She was in so much pain. Moaning. Barely breathing. Bleeding badly from her mouth and nose.

I stepped forward and knelt beside her and lifted her by her chin with one hand, and peeled the duct tape back with the other.

Looking at me, she stammered, "Y—you . . . f—fucking . . . b—b—bitch . . ."

I watched her for a few seconds, and then leaned forward and gave her what she'd given me in the hospital.

My regards, and a kiss on her lips.

I covered her mouth with the duct tape again and stood up and turned to the men I'd hired.

"The rest of the money is waiting for you."

The man from club said, "What do we do with her?"

I looked down at Kyra. She had no Fat Jim to save her.

I said, "She lives . . . she talks."

All three men nodded.

"Make sure the place is spotless when you're finished. I have buyers coming in the morning."

I turned and walked away.

Kyra screamed behind me.

I went back to the club to have another passion 'n pagne.

Future

She's good. Not as good as me, but good.

She's still a little rough around the edges. She hasn't grasped just how powerful she is yet. She knows she's got it, but there's still work to be done. But she's getting there.

Aida Stone.

I'd seen her months ago when I was at the 40/40 club waiting to take Kyra down. She'd been on the dance floor, holding a drink in her hand, moving to the music. She was alone and completely in her element. While Kyra was being seduced against the wall, I watched her. Watched her move. Watched her relish the attention she was commanding.

Coffee-colored skin. High end stripper's physique. Hair, Halle Berry short. Dressed in a knee-length, form-fitting black dress with spaghetti straps. Black pumps. Silver necklace with matching earrings. She was simple, yet fierce.

She reminded me of me.

I watched her for a few minutes after Kyra was led past me. Before I left to take care of my business, I approached her.

"You're good," I said. "But you still have a few things to learn about control."

She looked at me with feline eyes. Said, "Who the hell are you?"

I said, "I'll be back in an hour. If you'd like to learn what control is all about, you'll still be here."

I walked away and went to take care of Kyra. When I came back, she was sitting by the bar. I watched her turn down a celebrity most women would have done anything for. Not accustomed to rejection, he walked away pissed. I went and sat beside her.

"You're here by yourself. Why?"

She looked over at me. Her eyes were made for seduction. She said, "Why not?"

I nodded. That had been a good answer. "Are you a hooker?"

Her eyes became slits. Told me she was more dangerous than she let on. That was good too. She said, "No. Are you?"

I shook my head.

"Are you a lesbian? Because if you are, I don't swing that way."

I laughed. "No. I'm not."

She looked at me with those eyes. Wondered if I wasn't, then why had I approached her?

I said, "Are you married?"

She held up her hand. Showed me there was no ring.

"Boyfriend?"

"No boyfriend. No sugar daddy. I'm just doing me."

"Fuck who you want to fuck, when you want to fuck, right?"

"Exactly," she said. Her eyes told me that she'd never met anyone on her level before.

We stared at one another as the music thumped. We were both looking into mirrors. She was seeing an older, more sophisticated, more powerful version of herself. I was seeing myself without the proper guidance.

I said, "Why did you wait?"

"I had nothing better to do. Not yet anyway."

I smiled. I liked her. I reached into my purse and grabbed a pen and then a cocktail napkin. I wrote my number down on it and slid it toward her. "If you want to make money . . . call me."

She looked down at the napkin, then at me. "I told you, I'm no hooker." She slid the napkin back toward me.

I got up from the bar stool. "I'm not recruiting. Call me if you like to be in control." I walked away. The next day, she called.

"She's good," I told Marlene.

"But not as good as you."

"No," I said. "That's not possible."

Marlene smiled. "No, it's not."

Months after Kyra disappeared, we brought Aida into the business. I suppose I could have quit. I had money, and would for as long as Steve wanted to stay out of prison. Most women would have been satisfied with that. After everything that happened with Kyra, most women would have said they'd had enough. That they didn't want to risk getting into a situation like that again.

But I wasn't most women. What I'd gone through had only made me stronger. Being stronger made me more powerful. Being more powerful meant I had more control. Like Myles and his gambling, control was my addiction. I thrived on it. That would always be the thing that got me off the most.

Aida was brought into the business because, as it had been for me, her path had been pre-determined. My path brought me to Marlene. Aida's brought her to me. I didn't know what path was next. Only that it didn't make sense to stray away from it.

Home wrecker.
Some may not agree with the profession.
But many pay for the services.

Book Club Discussion Questions

1. Lisette—did you love or hate her?

2. How much do you think the relationship she had with her parents affect her?

3. Was Lisette's profession morally wrong?

4. Did Kyra get what she deserved?

5. Which character intrigued you the most?

6. Did the identity of the man in the black mask surprise you?

7. What was it about Lisette that made her so "powerful"?

8. Would you like to see Lisette again?

9.   What were your feelings about Myles?

10.   How far do you think Lisette takes her
      new career?

Conversation with Author Dwayne S. Joseph

Q: Home Wrecker. Wow! This was a very sexy and intense novel. Very different from your previous works. Why?

A: Thank you! I really just wanted to get away from doing just relationship drama. I don't want to get pigeonholed into doing one type of story only, because that would limit me as a writer, and that's just something I wanted to keep from happening.

Q: Well, you definitely got away from it! So tell us about Ms. Thang, Lisette. Where did she come from?

A: LOL. Ms. Thang. I like that. Lisette . . . she just came to me one day. I don't remember where I was or what I was doing, but she walked up to me and just told me that she was a home wrecker, and that I had no choice but to listen to her story. Lisette is my femme fatale. I had a lot of fun with her. She's sexy, fierce, arrogant, cold, at times even downright ignorant. You'll love her, hate her, and then love her all over again. Maybe hate her again too. I'm really going to miss her.

Q: Any chance of you bringing her back?

A: I don't really do sequels, but with the way the book ends, there may be some opportunities for her to reappear.

Q: The other characters in the book all had their own skeletons and twists to their personality. Why?

A: I just really wanted to present a dynamic group of characters who all had issues, as we all do, that would add a lot of different elements to the story. I like flawed characters. I think they're more memorable when they are flawed.

Q: Oh, everyone in this book is unforgettable, that's for sure. It was a great read!

A: Thank you!

Q: What's next for you?

A: I'm working on another intense novel, titled *Betrayal*.

Q: Looking forward to reading it! Thanks again and keep doing what you do!

A: Thank you. I will definitely do my best.

Notes

Notes

ORDER FORM
URBAN BOOKS, LLC
78 E. Industry Ct
Deer Park, NY 11729

Name: (please print):_____

Address:_____

City/State:_____

Zip:_____

QTY	TITLES	PRICE
	16 On The Block	$14.95
	A Girl From Flint	$14.95
	A Pimp's Life	$14.95
	Baltimore Chronicles	$14.95
	Baltimore Chronicles 2	$14.95
	Betrayal	$14.95
	Black Diamond	$14.95

Shipping and handling-add $3.50 for 1st book, then $1.75 for each additional book.
Please send a check payable to:
Urban Books, LLC
Please allow 4-6 weeks for delivery

ORDER FORM
URBAN BOOKS, LLC
78 E. Industry Ct
Deer Park, NY 11729

Name: (please print):_____

Address:_____

City/State:_____

Zip:_____

QTY	TITLES	PRICE
	Black Diamond 2	$14.95
	Black Friday	$14.95
	Both Sides Of The Fence	$14.95
	Both Sides Of The Fence 2	$14.95
	California Connection	$14.95
	California Connection 2	$14.95

Shipping and handling-add $3.50 for 1st book, then $1.75 for each additional book.
Please send a check payable to:
Urban Books, LLC
Please allow 4-6 weeks for delivery

ORDER FORM
URBAN BOOKS, LLC
78 E. Industry Ct
Deer Park, NY 11729

Name: (please print):_____

Address:_____

City/State:_____

Zip:_____

QTY	TITLES	PRICE
	Cheesecake And Teardrops	$14.95
	Congratulations	$14.95
	Crazy In Love	$14.95
	Cyber Case	$14.95
	Denim Diaries	$14.95
	Diary Of A Mad First Lady	$14.95
	Diary Of A Stalker	$14.95

Shipping and handling-add $3.50 for 1st book, then $1.75 for each additional book.
Please send a check payable to:
Urban Books, LLC
Please allow 4-6 weeks for delivery

ORDER FORM
URBAN BOOKS, LLC
78 E. Industry Ct
Deer Park, NY 11729

Name: (please print):_____

Address:_____

City/State:_____

Zip:_____

QTY	TITLES	PRICE
	Diary Of A Street Diva	$14.95
	Diary Of A Young Girl	$14.95
	Dirty Money	$14.95
	Dirty To The Grave	$14.95
	Gunz And Roses	$14.95
	Happily Ever Now	$14.95
	Hell Has No Fury	$14.95

Shipping and handling-add $3.50 for 1st book, then $1.75 for each additional book.

Please send a check payable to:

Urban Books, LLC

Please allow 4-6 weeks for delivery

ORDER FORM
URBAN BOOKS, LLC
78 E. Industry Ct
Deer Park, NY 11729

Name: (please print):_____

Address:_____

City/State:_____

Zip:_____

QTY	TITLES	PRICE
	Hush	$14.95
	If It Isn't love	$14.95
	Kiss Kiss Bang Bang	$14.95
	Last Breath	$14.95
	Little Black Girl Lost	$14.95
	Little Black Girl Lost 2	$14.95

Shipping and handling-add $3.50 for 1st book, then $1.75 for each additional book.
Please send a check payable to:
Urban Books, LLC
Please allow 4-6 weeks for delivery